THE CONVENT
OF THE PURE

THE CONVENT
OF THE PURE

Sara M. Harvey

AN APEX PUBLICATIONS BOOK
Lexington, Kentucky

THE CONVENT OF THE PURE

Copyright © 2009 by Sara M. Harvey
Cover Art "The Convent of the Pure" by Melissa Gay
Interior Art by Melissa Gay

Published by Apex Publications, LLC
PO Box 24323
Lexington, KY 40524

www.apexbookcompany.com
www.saramharvey.com
www.melissagay.com

First Edition, April 2009

ISBN: 978-0-0816390-9-3

Printed in the United States of America

10 9 8 7 6 5 4 3 2 1

To my readers, who have been nothing but supportive and kind, not to mention patient!

This book is for you. Yes, *you*.

"And it came to pass, when men began to multiply on the face of the earth, and daughters were born unto them, that the sons of God saw the daughters of men that they were fair; and they took them wives of all which they chose. The Nephilim were on the earth in those days, and also afterward, when the sons of God came unto the daughters of men, and they bare children to them, the same became mighty men which were of old, men of renown."

Genesis 6:1-2, 4

Lightning cracked the sky with a harsh, purple-white illumination. In its wake, a crisp tang of ozone and something deeper. Out of habit born of long training, Portia Gyony tasted the air, drawing in a deep lungful of breath through her mouth and nose at once. There it was, the sulphurous dark stench of brimstone.

"Careful now, he sees you." Imogen's voice was soft in her ear. Portia could only feel the spirit hovering just behind her right shoulder. She nodded and hoisted the crossbow with quivering arms. She fiddled with the brass tension dial, twisting it until it clicked and then some. "Relax and let your gifts work for you, don't force them."

"I don't think I can do this," Portia whispered. She had been so confident once, so vibrant and fearless.

"Of course you can," Imogen laughed, just as she had when she'd been alive, just as she had when she'd been Portia's partner in the flesh. "Now quickly, notch your bolt, he is getting ready to spring."

Imogen's hand was suddenly solid and firm on her shoulder, and Portia shot. She reloaded and shot again, striking her small but vicious target with a heavy, wet *throk* followed by a scream that would have turned her hair stark silver-white if that hadn't already happened to her years ago. Portia drew in a shuddering breath, realizing only then that she'd been holding it. She strode forward through the thick ground fog. There, about twenty feet ahead, was the writhing body of the fiend. Fiends were hideous little imps with ravaged red flesh twisted and thickened like it had been horribly burnt. She loaded another bolt and fired it directly into the thing's conical head. It erupted in acrid blue-green flames, and Portia refused to step back from it, even though the stench was abysmal. When the flames had died to hot, oily ashes, she scraped the fetid matter into a lead cylinder.

"Well done, my dear." Imogen's voice died into the breath of wind, and after one last petulant crack of thunder, the storm also cleared and Portia found herself entirely alone.

The chapter house was mostly dark when Portia arrived. She checked her pocket watch and found that it was well past midnight. The flickering gaslights in the library were, of course, lit. Since coming to this rambling mansion as a child, she had never seen that room dim. She brought her motorized cycle sputtering to a halt in the front roundabout. It had been a lonely ride home without Imogen's comforting presence, but the ghost had pushed herself hard out there. Becoming solid took a great deal of exertion, not to mention the scouting Imogen had been doing beyond sight. Portia was eager to get inside where Imogen could speak to her with greater ease. She swung her battered leather Gladstone bag over her shoulder and shifted her corset into a more comfortable position. It was a new, modern accoutrement with the latest in spring steel and real elastic, but the damn thing still rode up on her. She

kicked the dust from her boots before slipping into the elegant but forbidding chapter house.

"You are not coming in without giving report, are you?" Lady Hester's voice stopped her cold in her tracks. The headmistress had not even bothered to look up from her desk at the far side of the library. Lady Hester belonged to the Edulica sect of educators and governesses, charged by the Primacy of the Grigori with finding promising children and teaching them their true Nephilim heritage and purpose. She was a strong, graceful woman with thick golden hair only just starting to grey at the edges. She looked hale for being one hundred and eight years old. She had raised Portia and her fellows and had then gone into semi-retirement, overseeing her chapter house, keeping tabs on prospects, and reporting to the Primacy.

Portia paused in the doorway. At twenty-four, she was only a few months shy of her age of majority, but Lady Hester could make her feel like a child caught stealing from the cookie jar. "Might it wait until morning?"

Hester turned and pushed her tiny gold-rimmed glasses up onto her regal forehead. "No," was all she said. It was all she needed to say.

Portia nodded, defeated, and shuffled into the library. She felt the weight of the night's long ordeal on her shoulders, and in the warm glow of the library's gaslights, she could see that she had singed the hem of her duster. She sighed and dug the leather-wrapped lead cylinder out of her satchel. She all but dropped it on the desk.

Hester dropped her glasses back onto her nose and gazed at the cylinder. "What was it?"

"Fiend."

"Did it incinerate on its own or did you need to burn it?"

"Went right up when I put a Blessedwood stake in its head."

She nodded at the dirty case sitting on her spotless desk. "All of it is in here?"

"Enough of it, yeah." Portia crossed her arms and stifled a yawn.

Hester folded her hands, hiding the tremor of temper in her fingers. "Portia, please."

Portia looked away, staring instead at the dark line of burnt cotton at the edge of the tan canvas of her coat. She hated few things in life more than apologizing. She drew a deep breath and put on her best and most sincerely contrite expression. "I am sorry, ma'am. I'm just tired. May I be excused to a bath and to bed, please?"

Hester nodded but cleared her throat sharply. "One last thing."

"Yes?"

"Was Imogen with you?" The question hung between them.

Hester's gaze was penetrating, and Portia often wondered why the headmistress asked after Imogen night after night. Did Lady Hester harbor any enmity toward her for Imogen's death? Hester's face was inscrutable.

Portia lifted her chin and returned the Lady's cool comportment. "Imogen is always with me."

Hester tilted her head and regarded Portia a long moment before scratching out a note with her fountain pen. "You may go," she said absently.

* * *

Portia's room was at the farthest corner away from the library, with a south-facing window looking out over the Blessedwood orchard. Once the door was shut, she sensed a familiar flurry of perfumed air around her. The bedroom had become Imogen's haven. Portia kept a small trunk of Imogen's most cherished possessions, and being near such comfortable and safe surroundings seemed to give the spirit strength. Within heartbeats, beside the bed appeared a beautiful young woman with rich red hair and deep olivine eyes flecked with gold. She looked solid, human, and alive. It was an illusion. Imogen Gyony had been dead for two years.

"You did well tonight," Imogen said, all charm and grace. She hopped up and nearly danced across the room toward Portia. She stole a kiss and pulled the faded indigo kerchief off of Portia's head. Silver tresses tumbled down over Portia's shoulders, and with glad effort, Imogen ran her fingers through their ethereal curls. Portia never let anyone else touch her hair. She hated it. She'd shaved it more than once and dyed it a hundred times, but no matter what she used, no color ever stuck to it. The other children of the chapter house had mocked her for it; even Lady Hester had been less than kind.

Her hair had been light as a child, she remembered, but had darkened as she'd grown, becoming a deep auburn. But as she grew into adolescence, it had begun to pale again, turning nearly tow-blonde as it had been when she'd been but a lass. At seventeen she had been considered old enough to endure her trials and was sent out to hunt her first demon. Alone on her birthday, as soon as it was dark. To track and destroy a demon in combat would prove her worthiness to join the Gyony, the warrior sect. The demon had been a fiend. She had defeated it, but the soul-piercing death cry had brought her to her knees. And when she had risen to collect its damnable ashes, she'd found that her hair had turned silvery white. It shamed her, and she kept it as secret as she could.

Imogen twirled a lock of Portia's hair around her ethereal fingers. "Now that it's done, you can never be hurt that way again, you realize. You are invulnerable to fiends and shock-sprites and any number of ghastly ghouls." Her vaporous lips were playful against Portia's cheek.

Portia shook herself free of the spirit's touch. She was in no mood to be cheered or seduced. "I am not happy with my performance tonight. I made some stupid mistakes. I froze up."

"You worry too much. You always worry too much! But I suppose if you didn't, then you wouldn't be my beloved—" Imogen froze, fear widening her eyes. "He's coming!" Her voice was all but swallowed in the rush of light and breath as she vanished.

The door swung open and Nigel Aldias strolled in as if it were his own room. "Good evening, sweet foster-sister. Back late, I see."

Portia's back stiffened and she met his eyes with unblinking assurance. "Since when do you just waltz into my quarters?"

Nigel's dark grey gaze flitted across the room, pausing specifically on Portia's hair. His mouth bent into a derisive half-smile. She fumed. He had not and would not ever let her live that mistake down, nor any other. Especially not the one that had cost Imogen her life. His nostrils flared and his grey eyes narrowed. "You've had company. I smell a lady's sweet perfume." After a deep and showy inhale, he chuckled. "Ah, yes, the scent of lilies, so precious to the *dead*."

"Why are you here?"

Nigel sat down on the corner of her bed and crossed his long, elegant legs. He'd been found on the front steps of the chapter house in a hatbox, but he had grown from an abandoned infant into a powerful necromancer and was already a ranking member in the House of Aldias. Nigel was a prodigy; he was still three years away from his majority and two years Portia's junior. But the Aldias, the sect of magic-users who fought with unseen powers rather than with their own hands, did not seem to care. They had a habit of assuming that the rules did not apply to them. The Gyony thought poorly of the Aldias. The feeling was mutual.

Nigel's smile was a contemptible mockery of affection. "Do I need a reason to come and visit you, foster-sister?"

He was oily. And Portia owed him a favor, a big one. It was Nigel who had ensnared Imogen's soul, tying it to the mortal realm using the strength of her celestial heritage. Imogen was able to remain by Portia's side among the living, but she was terrified of Nigel and his tricks. She refused to be anywhere near him, mostly in case he changed his mind. Portia could not blame her in the slightest and also avoided Nigel's company as best she could.

"I had a rough night, Nigel. Can we revisit this social call over breakfast tomorrow, perhaps?"

He picked at something invisible on his immaculately manicured fingernails. "Oh, I suppose." He sighed and searched Portia's face, looking so burdened and so penitent. Portia was immediately on guard. "Dear foster-sister, I have been thinking…. What do you think would happen to this chapter house if something were to become of Hester?"

"*Lady* Hester," Portia corrected testily.

He spread his hands in a gesture that might have been mistaken for an apology by someone who had never before met him. "You have not answered my question, Portia, my sweet."

"I honestly say I have never thought about it."

"Haven't you? Really? An ambitious lass like yourself, I am surprised!"

"Spill it, Nigel, or so help me, I will scream for Emile and have you removed."

He looked affronted. "That would be awfully rude. And after I have been so good to you. And to your beloved Imogen." When he saw that Portia was listening, he continued. "My point is this: Lady Hester Edulica is retired from her recruiting and educational responsibilities. I have seen the Primacy missives that all but dismiss her from duty. The few of us who remain in this house will be twenty-five soon and entitled to leave our fosterage. And then, what shall become of the place?" He glanced about, the feigned pity was all but carved into his face. "The library, the resources, the orchard. It should be maintained by the Primacy. Or by a worthy replacement."

Portia shook her head, chasing the weariness from her mind. She yawned widely. "So, that's all? You came up here in the middle of the night to say that you want me to support you to take over the chapter house when Lady Hester retires?"

He tilted his head, as if carefully considering her words. Surprisingly, he smiled. "Yes." He nodded and rose to his feet, sweeping a lock of dark hair behind his ear. "Yes, that is what I am asking you. Can I count on your support? We have always been so close, you and I. And you know there is nothing that I would *ever* refuse you." He touched a lock of Portia's hair.

Portia winced at the intimate gesture and brushed his fingers away. "Sure, Nigel. When, and *if* the time comes, I will do what I can. I doubt it shall mean much. Neither of us are Edulica. You'll have a tough time convincing the Primacy that an Aldias should have the care of *children*."

He shrugged. "Those are details to be dealt with later. But for now, we are agreed, then?" He offered his hand.

"We are agreed that I will help you in whatever limited capacity that I am able should the situation ever present itself." She placed her hand in his, and his fingers clasped hers like a vice. She shivered as he held her, pinned both by his powerful grip and his penetrating stare. Something shimmered darkly in his eyes.

"Oh, Portia, I knew I could count on you. I knew you would want to help me. You can see more than the others can, you can see the shape of the future." His voice was filled with elation just as his eyes were filled with danger. He drew her close and Portia could feel his well-muscled thigh beneath his tweed trousers. She tensed, preparing to defend herself when he kissed her cheek and released her.

Portia's knees turned to rubber and she sat down hard,

sinking into the down coverlet of her bed. Adrenaline seared her veins, and she fought off a wave of dizziness. When she opened her eyes, the door to the corridor was standing open and Nigel was gone. Imogen hovered beside her, flickering and nervous.

"He is up to no good," Imogen whispered fiercely, casting a fretful glance into the hallway. "Are you well, my love?"

Portia could only nod and clasp her hands together to keep them from shaking. "Well enough." She summoned the strength to stand and go shut the door. Leaning heavily against it, she could not begin to comprehend what terrible machinations Nigel might have planned. And she had just promised him her aid in them. "What have I done?"

The Nephilim took the promise of aid quite seriously and had always done so since the dawn of recorded history. They believed themselves to be the bridge between the mortal plane and the celestial, the bond between earth and heaven. Even in the modern age of steam-engines and skepticism, they heralded themselves as angelic champions, the protectors of mankind. They allowed condemnation upon their heads and were called monster, corruptor, wicked. They were a tall and fearsome people with a terrible beauty well documented in the Old Testament. But in order to truly serve their divine purpose, they knew they must do so in secret. The Nephilim allowed the myth of the Great Flood to drown them, to wash them away from history and memory. They retreated into the shadows of the world and were said to reside in a deep and hidden valley until the Day of Judgment when God would call them forth and, presumably, condemn them. But Judgment Day was a long way off, and humanity was still so tender and fallible. With great pathos and pity, they decided amongst themselves to emerge from their hidden places and their shrouded ways and build a society with the sole purpose of being the sword, shield, and blessing of humanity. They became the *Grigori*, the Watchers. They worked in secret to stand against the great powers of darkness and evil. They divided into sects built from family-clans to better divide the monumental undertaking of protecting all of mankind. The Grigori were not so covert as to go entirely unnoticed, so the ones most clever when it came to misdirection and the arcane made certain to push the tales to the farthest edges of legend. The idea of the Grigori, even the very concept of Nephilim, was relegated to the *Apocrypha* and the late-night tale-spinnings of old women by the fire. In truth, the actual Grigori spread out across the face of the earth, multiplying and growing stronger under the watchful care of the Primacy. Concealed by the shadows of myth, they fought a pitched battle against the adversaries of men and women so that all of humanity could be at peace.

Or so Portia had been taught as a child. She had come to this particular chapter house at the age of seven, an auspicious number and the standard age to begin training. It was essential to find children of Nephilim heritage before they began to exhibit strange and disturbing powers, and before they ceased to age or began to mature inappropriately. Portia had been brought from her small town, two days' carriage ride away, to the quiet, rustic village of Penemue, at the center of which was the great house. It was a locale almost removed from the world with its clean-swept cobblestone streets and rosy-cheeked residents. They were a tall people, full of grace and awe-inspiring beauty. No one had looked askance at Portia, who had grown before her time and at age seven had more than once fended off a lustful hand reaching for a pinch.

Penemue was a haven for all the children. There were barnyards full of goats and chickens and cats. There were orchards full of apples and pears and plums. There were ponds and streams and meadows. And every single man, woman, and child bore the unmistakable stamp of the Nephilim on every inch of their bodies. Even if a child was not suitable for training as an active member of the Grigori, they were still brought into the village, nestled in a low-lying valley filled with wildflowers and vineyards, to be raised among their own kind. Lady Hester ran the village as surely as she controlled the chapter house, and instilled a love of it so deep in the hearts of the residents that there was no hesitation to defend it, even to the death. The Gyony had at first resisted adopting members from the village, thinking them soft and useless in battle, but they were wrong. The children of Penemue made some of the most excellent warriors. They had a certain passion that only came from fighting for something dearly loved.

It had been a charmed life, a carefree existence. Portia remembered so clearly the day she and Imogen had their first kiss, in the market square behind the apple seller's

booth. Their lips had been sticky and sweet with juice.
And there was the day down by the stream when they'd
splashed and swum and stretched out on the bankside
rocks to dry in the hot summer sun. Imogen deserved a
better fate. Imogen should have been the one valiantly
slaying demons and ghouls, full of life and beauty and
power. Portia would have traded places with her in a moment; she would have been content to exist as a spirit, a
guardian angel at her lover's side. She would have given
anything to repeat that night and never take her eyes off
of Imogen, not for an instant.

"Portia?" She jolted at the voice. Emile Edulica leaned
over her with a tea tray. "Portia, lass? What will you? Tea,
coffee? Sugar, milk? I can't hold this up all day." He was
handsome and had to be nearly one hundred years old,
but still full of youthful vigor and delightfully angled
cheekbones, with toffee-brown hair swept back in a low
ponytail. He was Hester's heir-apparent, should she ever
decide to officially retire and leave it all to him. But the
Primacy had not sent Hester or Emile on any new scouting forays in over a year. It was unsettling to them, Portia
knew, but they hid it behind placid smiles and went about
their daily tasks as if nothing were amiss.

"Tea, please. Sugar, no milk." Portia still remembered
when she'd first seen him, stepping out of the carriage in
front of her parents' house and opening the door for Hester. After the long ride from her parents' lonely house,
Emile had carried her in his arms into the Penemue chapter house, up the stairs into her new room and her new

life. She had mistaken him for a servant, then. Even now, it was easy to forget that this man with his calming, quiet manners and tendency to dote was really her superior while she lived at Penemue. He set her cup before her and seated himself in the chair opposite.

"Daydreaming again, I see."

She shrugged. "Just strolling down memory lane. How are you today?"

He glanced aside before answering. "I am well."

"You are lying."

Emile's eyes were usually the color of a perfectly blue spring sky, but they turned a peculiar color when he was troubled or angry. They were a pale periwinkle now, nearly violet. He looked openly around the sitting room. One of the maids was sweeping up and a squat clockwork assistant was clattering behind her, dutifully holding up a dustbin. Emile clapped his hands and made a gentle shooing gesture, and the maid bobbed him a curtsey and left the room with the little wheeled clockwork on her heels, its dustbin tucked away to be emptied somewhere else. The maid even paused to close the pocket doors behind her, leaving Portia alone in the sitting room with Emile. For a few long moments, there was no sound but the crackling of the fire laid in the fireplace to ward off the chill still hanging in the early spring air.

"The Lady is ill," he said softly, as if the very admission of it might do Hester further injury.

"Ill? How?"

He shook his head, and Portia thought she saw tears gathering in his eyes. "I am not sure. I went to look in on her this morning and I could not wake her. She's pale and her breath is ragged. Sometimes she sweats and sometimes she shivers." He scratched nervously at the back of his neck. "She has been like this all day."

"She seemed fine last night. A little tired, maybe, but certainly nothing more serious than that!"

"When did you see her?"

"It was late. Nearly one, I think. I brought my report to her in the library when I got back from my assignment."

He nodded. "Was anyone else awake when you got in?"

Portia began to shake her head, then remembered her cryptic meeting with the necromancer. "Nigel was awake," she told him. She despaired of saying anything further, knowing that somehow he would find out.

Emile did not press, as if he, too, realized the potential danger. "I should look in on Lady Hester. I have sent word about her illness, but I have received no answer from the Primacy. Lady Claire Aldias is on her way up from the village with Miniver Sweetwater, the midwife. I don't know what else I should do."

Portia nodded, feigning a calm she did not feel. "Do you think that is necessary? I am certain Lady Hester will be fine." Her heart raced. Somehow, this was all playing right into Nigel's plans. Lady Claire was a renowned healer, but she was an Aldias and Portia feared Nigel's influence.

"She needs to be seen by a healer," Emile said firmly, his words cracking just slightly. In his strained voice, Portia heard the terrifying truth of the severity of Lady Hester's condition.

Her mouth went dry. "Emile, if things get any worse,

please alert me. If you wouldn't mind?" She added the last hastily, hoping he would not suspect that she knew more than she was telling. But Emile was distraught, he noticed nothing but his own fear.

He stood, bumping the table and rattling the tea set. He opened his mouth to speak, but Dinah, the head maid, came bustling in. Although she was in a terrible rush, she still paused to curtsey deeply and beg forgiveness for the interruption.

"Mistress Portia, you are needed. It is urgent." She held out the hastily transcribed message. It had been a telegraph wire transmission, Portia could tell by the syntax. Those were hit and miss in terms of the kind of enemy and the location. It was terrible timing. And Portia did not think it was entirely coincidental. There was nothing to be done but investigate.

"Emile, would you please excuse me?"

He glanced up, having sat himself down again and begun staring at the tea set as if he had never seen it before. She hated to leave him alone, but Lady Claire and the midwife would be there shortly. He stood again and gave her an awkward embrace. "Of course. Take care, lass. And hurry home."

Portia's things were always at the ready. Her satchel held her favorite crossbow and a quiver of smooth, ivory-colored Blessedwood bolts. A jar of holy water and a pouch of herbs and incense were nestled in a side pocket along with a handful of silver medallions strung on leather cords. A half-dozen lead canisters clinked together, rolling over a well-worn map of the area and a bronze compass with a badly scratched cover. She threw her battered duster on over her sensible shirtwaist and divided skirt and twirled her silver braid hastily on top of her head before tying a faded paisley kerchief over it. She stuffed her new wireless transmitter into her pocket; although it was a piece of top-of-the-line technology, it was still less than trustworthy. Its range was limited, but she could usually raise another member of the Grigori or even a police bobby if the situation was dire.

   She was back downstairs in moments, but Emile was already gone. The library door was ajar, and for the first time since she had come to Penemue more than seventeen years ago, the library was dark.

   Portia moved quickly across the lawn and was nearly running by the time she reached the far end of the roundabout. Her motorized cycle was waiting for her in the garage, and so was Imogen. She watched quietly as Portia donned her helmet and gunned the motor.

   "It is worse than you think," Imogen said.

   "I think it's pretty terrible, actually." Portia leaped onto the cycle. "Can you tell me on the way?"

   The spirit nodded and slipped behind her. Her misty arms wrapped around Portia's body and memories came. Portia longed for nothing more than to lose herself in them and forget the troubles that haunted her. But duty called and she forced the dazzle of nostalgic tears from her eyes so she could focus on the road.

   "You must be careful of Nigel. The House of Aldias has fed his ambition too much."

"Tell me something I didn't know. Is he responsible for Lady Hester?"

Imogen paused, considering. "If he is, I cannot say how. But I would not doubt it. That is no ordinary illness she has, I can tell that much." Her voice was beyond Portia's ears now, it was inside her mind. "But we must take care tonight. We are running directly toward danger."

"Should I not have left the chapter house?"

"It wouldn't have mattered." The resignation in her words made her sound old and tired. "What is coming for you will find you no matter what."

2

T he address was difficult to find. More than
once, Portia consulted her map. She'd made
good time on the road in from Penemue, but once in the
city she'd made wrong turn after wrong turn until it was
dark. Imogen was silent the entire time; even when Portia
begged her to scout ahead, she remained where she was
with her spectral arms wrapped around Portia's waist.
Frustrated, Portia stopped a fruit-seller dragging his lopsided cart toward the small bridge that spanned the river.

He looked at the address, but only laughed when she
asked him to point it to her on the map.

"You won'ta find that on no map. That place been
closed down since who-knows-when. Used to be a nunnery, or a 'ospital, mebbe. Don't rightly remember now.
'Twas a long time ago." He huffed and carefully set his
cart handles down onto the grimy cobblestones. "Now
y'see here this road we're on? Follows the river. You keep
a-goin' 'til you come 'round to 'nother bridge. A big one.
Now, don'ta go over that bridge. You go away from it.
Keep the water at your back, and you remember to come
home to it later, unnerstan'?"

Portia nodded when it was apparent that he would not
continue unless given some acknowledgement that she

did indeed "unnerstan'." "I follow this road to a large bridge. Turn left and go away from the river."

"You pick up quick. You pretty ones always worry me, all the power's in the looks and none in the brains. But what was I sayin'? Oh, yes. Away from the water, up the hill. The road gives out but the path don't. Keep on until you pick up the road again and it'lla lead you right to the gates of that place. 'Course, you mightaswell be walkin' up to the gates of Hell."

"Thanks. I appreciate the help."

"You take care now, missy. Here, take one for the road. Some days, that road up there gets mighty long. Can'ta figure out how. But when I used to sell fruit to the nuns at the wall, there was some days it'd take me clear half the day just getting' there. Strangest thing I ever did see." He put a large yellow apple into her hand. It was heavy and ripe with only one brown oval bruise on it. The man hefted the cart again and shifted his weight to get it moving once more. "You take care now. Don'ta be getting' yourself kill'd. Cryin' shame when a pretty girl gets herself kill'd. Happens all t'time. Dunno what this world's comin' to. Pretty girl can'ta hardly walk down the streets without puttin' herself right in middle of trouble." He continued to mutter to himself as the cart creaked and rattled away over the narrow bridge.

Portia watched him go. "You do realize what this means, don't you?" she whispered to Imogen.

The spirit nodded. "The place on the hill is shrouded. I can sense it even here. The power there is not one of Grigori origin, but based off of Grigori teachings."

"Is it demon magic, then?"

"No, not exactly. It is a muddle of things, part Nephilim magic, part demonmancery. We shouldn't go there alone. We shouldn't go there at all, in fact."

"I can't very well ignore a summons and you know that. Someone there has asked for our help; duty and honor demand we at least investigate."

Imogen was silent and invisible a long moment. Finally, Portia felt the whisper of incorporeal lips against her earlobe. "Then I shall protect you as best I can, my love."

Portia's eyes closed as she tried to blot out the unbidden memories of when it had been she that had promised Imogen that very same thing. Such had her protection been. Portia sighed and nodded, not trusting her voice to speak. She gunned the engine and jumped when it backfired, sending a spray of steam and sparks into the air behind them.

The road was just as the fruit-peddler had described. When they arrived at the large masonry bridge, Portia turned to the low hill rising up beside the road. The paving grew more and more decrepit as they ascended, finally ending in an expanse of rubble strewn through the stubby grass. A double trail formed by cart or automobile wheels pressed on through the mess of broken cobblestones and past the trees, still skeletal with their winter boughs. The buildings had given way blocks before, as if the very architecture had retreated away from the ominous and chilling aura that rolled off the hilltop like fog.

"Let's go," Portia said resolutely. She rummaged around the Gladstone bag and pulled out one of the medallions. "Christopher, Denied Saint, it is you that I still venerate. Whoever shall behold the image of Saint Christopher shall not faint or fall on that day. I beseech you, guide my steps, allow me safe travel to my destination and home again."

She dropped the necklace over her head and kissed the smooth, cool silver before slipping it beneath her shirtwaist. The cycle's engine growled as she coasted through one of the rutted tracks. She watched the path ahead, not looking left or right, only gazing steadfastly toward her target. She could feel the magic around them; she could nearly smell it. Imogen held fast to her, burying her face against Portia's neck so she could not be distracted by the glamours that surrounded them. She, a creature of pure spirit, was especially susceptible. After about a hundred yards, the road began again. Not cobbles, but smooth, flat paving stones, each over ten feet wide and laid seamlessly alongside its neighbor, built a perfectly smooth road surface that ran in a straight line to an enormous gate.

Portia let the engine sputter into silence and pushed the cycle the last of the way. The gates looked old. They were ornate, with curved, vine-like designs and a tall archway from which hung a broken lantern. There were words on the archway: *The tongue of the righteous is choice silver, but the heart of the wicked is of little value.*

"Proverbs," Imogen said aloud.

"Creepy." Portia gazed at the intricate lettering full of flourishes and rust.

The gates were ajar and a thick chain was coiled on the ground between them, right beside a broken padlock. Although the gates were rusty and ill-used, the chain and padlock were gleaming and new. Portia loaded the crossbow, cranking the tiny brass knob with a series of tinny clicks. She pushed the gate with a booted foot. It squealed in protest before finally groaning open. She proceeded carefully. The area within the walls was quite unadorned, a wide parade ground flanked by long, low buildings. Vines had once grown along the walls and the sides of the buildings, but now they were only scraggly dead branches and black traceries that remained on the stone surfaces like scars. The main structure loomed at the far side of it, imposing in the darkness. Only a little moonlight fell, casting a pale glow that hid more than it illuminated.

"Which way?" Portia squinted into the darkness. The building to the right was boarded up and she could not see many details. It seemed square and utilitarian, like a storage area. To the left was an open corridor, only semi-enclosed by a series of Romanesque arches. It connected the central building with what appeared to be a chapel. "Let's start there."

Imogen followed, gazing with Portia up at the large edifice that dominated the compound. The bottommost floors had been constructed from a light brown stone with striking yellow veining. There were floral carvings above the entries and various other reliefs obscured by shadow. Each progressive floor seemed to have been added on, bearing its own architectural style and a composition that was not entirely congruous with the levels below and above it. It was not an altogether pleasing aesthetic. Portia was in no hurry to see what the interior looked like. Besides, if there were demons about, they were bound to be haunting the chapel anyway. They were dreadfully predictable that way.

The side door to the chapel was closed but not locked. Portia gently nudged it open, praying that the hinges were good. Inside, it was completely dark, and she could see where someone had gone in and painted the stained glass windows with opaque black. It raised the hair on the back of her neck. She reached for a piece of resin incense from her pack.

"Lucifer, bearer of light, you seek atonement. Aid me in slaying your misbegotten kin. Take what repentance you may, be my guide, bring me light, allow me to see. Fallen One, this I command you." The resin lit up at once, casting a soft, orange glow like candlelight, yet remaining cool in her hand. The chapel was cloaked in a heavy layer of dust. The altar lay bare, devoid of all ritual trappings.

Portia moved forward carefully, conscious of the footprints she was leaving behind her. Closer to the altar, she could see that the floor there had been recently cleaned. Meticulously so, in fact. The scent of blood lingered in the air, almost overpowered by the harsh smell of lye soap. No mere human would have detected it, but to her, the odor of sacrifice was unmistakable. And recent.

"It was certainly human," Imogen confirmed. "This mischief was probably committed at sunset. Look, the altar is still wet."

Portia stretched her light toward it, careful not to get too close, and found that the dark graining of the surface was not a character of the wood or a tribute to its age, but where something had soaked into it. She dared not step into the cleaned area to investigate further. Instead, she crouched down and blew a sharp breath at the dusty border. Her suspicions were confirmed. A deep gouge scored the floor, creating a complete circle around the altar. The marking was old, but had recently been renewed. Whatever was happening up on this hill, she was certain it had been going on for decades, if not centuries. She began to wonder why they had never been called to investigate it before.

"What are you sensing? Are we alone here?"

Imogen winked out of Portia's vision briefly, then returned with a nod of her head. "Yes, for the moment, we are. There is something lurking here, but not in the chapel." She nodded toward the rear door, the one that opened onto the arched passageway.

"We should check the sacristy first, and then move on to the main building." Portia carefully edged around the ritual circle, making for the small preparation room behind the altar. Imogen followed, having neither agreed nor disagreed, but she seemed troubled. "You don't like it here, do you?"

"No," the ghost answered. "I did not want to come here."

Portia smiled. "But you did."

"I stay by your side, my love. It is my sworn duty."

"Thank you. I know I could face this alone, but everything is so much easier when we are together." She longed to reach out and squeeze Imogen's fingers, but those days were gone. Only on rare occasions could she become that solid. Instead, Portia could only share a caress with the glimmering air beside her. "Let's get to the bottom of this so we can go home."

Portia had her hand on the doorknob of the sacristy when the wireless transmitter in her pocket crackled to life. She jumped back, heart pounding, and nearly stum-

bled into the wretched circle. A buzz of static and a series
of clicks came chattering through the instrument. It
sounded like thunder in the tiny, quiet chapel. She shoved
it deeper into the pocket of her duster, closing her hand
around it to muffle the sound. But it was relentless, growing louder and louder until Portia pulled it out to turn it
off. The transmitter was a silly invention of one of her
classmates', meant to be able to send telegraphed code between members of a scouting party. It was unobtrusive,
small, and lightweight enough to carry in a pocket, and
relatively quiet. It had never before made the cacopho-
nous racket it was currently emitting. And then it did
something Portia had never thought physically possible. It
began to transmit a *voice*. A woman's eerie, silky voice.
The words faded in and out of hearing, crackling and hiss-
ing with static.

"They lie with the warriors, the Nephilim of old, who
descend to Sheol with their weapons of war."

The interference was tremendous, but the transmitter
refused to turn off. The indicator light dimmed, but each
time the woman spoke, it flickered to life again, bringing
her voice with it in a swell of volume. The waves of sound
climaxed and faded, but the words were muddled. The
voice seemed to upset Imogen especially, causing her to
flicker in and out of Portia's field of vision.

The chapel had been picked over. Nothing much remained that might have hinted that it had once been a
place of worship, only the altar, which was obviously being used for more nefarious purposes than celebrating the
Mass. Everything else had been removed, right down to
the tiny crucifixes that had adorned each row of pews. She

could see where they had been affixed and where they had been pried off, in some places with hasty and jagged tool marks that left deep scrapes in the wood.

As they neared the large door to the main building, the transmitter signal abruptly cleared. Portia could hear the woman now without any hindrance. For a long moment, there was only the sound of her breathing.

"Count us not amongst the Dead, look for us not below the Earth. We shall walk in sunlight, we shall purge the blood of the Daughters of Men from our veins, we shall claim our heritage as descendants of the most holy God! Bene 'elim! We claim our birthright! As Bene 'elim, we sing praises to the Most High! Amen! Amen! Amen!"

The transmitter light twinkled a moment, then went dark as the signal dissipated. Portia exchanged a worried glance with Imogen. She began to feel a cold thread of fear tugging at her as she realized that whoever had summoned them there was inside…and waiting for them.

3

Imogen had never spoken much about her past, not even with Portia. But Portia knew her beloved had been born in this city, and after her mother's suicide, Imogen had been taken to a convent to be raised. Imogen gave no real indication that this place might be familiar to her as they entered through the wide, arched door at the far end of the corridor. Inside was a cloak room, a narrow and poorly lit chamber full of sinister shadows that the resin's fitful light did nothing to dispel.

Light spilled in from around the interior door, and Portia opened it a crack to peer into the passageway beyond. She felt Imogen's cool hand on the back of her neck and jumped.

"Don't be afraid. I will be with you the entire time."

Portia nodded and pressed the door fully open. The hall before her was most certainly a part of the original construction of the convent, simple and sturdy, made with smooth, tawny stone. Along the center of the corridor's floor was a wide indentation made by centuries of shuffling feet moving to and from the chapel. She could almost hear soft footfalls and murmuring voices. It would have been a peaceful place, but the ugly electric bulbs installed overhead cast a garish light through the whole passage.

The hall emptied into a large central chamber with a vaulted ceiling, where Portia could detect the scent of blood once more. It drifted down from the second floor, roiling over the railings and down the stairs, distractingly fresh and pungent.

"What's up there?"

Imogen's shadowy form tensed. "Why do you think I should know?"

"Just a hunch."

The ghost sighed but did not even look up before she answered. "Up the stairs to our left were the nun's cells. To our right were dormitories. Between them were a series of large interconnected rooms that served as classrooms. More classrooms, playrooms, and dormitories were on the upper floors, but we mostly used them for storage. On this floor, there was a kitchen and a dining hall. And the chambers and offices of the Mother Superior."

"So, you were raised here."

Imogen nodded. "A long time ago. It was a true cloister, kept by the very sweet and very human Sisterhood of the Daughters of Men, with walls that enclosed us, keeping the wicked world at bay. No one was supposed to find us. Not even the Grigori..." Her form flickered like ripples on a pond as she trailed off.

"Are you going to be—"

"Fine? Yes. Yes, I will be just fine." She pointed up the stairs. "The dormitories. That is where the blood is coming from."

"Do you catch anything else? Demons? Ghosts? Humans?"

She shook her head. "No. The blood is too strong. And

the memories."

Portia ached to hold her, to wrap her arms around her and kiss her and kiss her until Imogen could think of nothing more than pleasure. She passed her solid hands through her lover's shimmering body. "I love you."

Imogen stepped away from her touch. "This way." She brushed her incorporeal hands across her face as if dashing away invisible tears. She vanished and reappeared halfway up the broad stairs to the second floor. "Portia, come."

Portia adjusted her bag across her shoulders and followed her lover up the steps and into Imogen's childhood home.

Imogen directed her into the first corridor they encountered. The smell of blood was overpowering. A balcony hugged the interior wall and wrapped all the way around to a matching corridor, mirrored directly across from them. Portia hoped they would not have to investigate that other wing—the thought of crossing that open walkway made her nervous. She turned to the door before her. It was locked. She began to prepare a spell when Imogen stopped her.

"Wait. There is an easier way. Do you have a hair pin?"

Portia tugged one of the pins from her coiled braid. She could see the intense concentration on Imogen's face as she became solid enough to take the pin and jiggle it into the keyhole. Her red-gold brows knit in deep concentration as she focused on picking the lock.

"It locks with a key; you need it to open the door from the outside *or* the inside. We used to do this all the time as children, you know, sneak out. Not like there was any place to go, really. But we did it anyway. Hellions, we were." She glanced back toward Portia with a wink. For an instant, they were their old selves again, mischievous and conspiring together. But that cheerful nostalgia faded when the lock clicked open and the silver hairpin fell to the floor. Portia was alone on the landing.

She eased open the door. Behind her, Imogen was flickering in and out of sight. It was dark within. The scent of blood was overwhelmed by the stench of iodine and ether. There was a faint rattling and clicking within the room and the sound of a chorus of breath rising and falling in eerie regularity. The light of the resin was fading, and Portia put it in the pocket of her duster. Lifting her crossbow into place, she nocked a bolt and turned the brass knob until it was ready to fire. The rhythmic breathing continued, relentless.

Her eyes slowly adjusted to the room, and faint outlines and shapes came into view. Row after row of narrow beds came into focus, with contraptions at the foot of each one. The metal boxes were attached to the end of each bed with wires that vanished beneath the thin, ragged blankets. Beneath each blanket lay a child, flat on its back. They were tall, with high cheekbones and luminous skin but shadowed, sunken eyes that flickered and twitched in restless dreams. Their hair had grown out over the pillows and hung over the sides of the beds. The machines attached to the children whirred and beeped and blinked tiny red and yellow lights, each one connected to a series of cloth-covered wires that snaked across the floor, disappearing into the gloom beyond. The only movements were the rising and falling of scrawny chests and the flutter of pallid eyelids.

Behind Portia, Imogen gasped. She was clearly visible now, and more agitated than Portia had ever seen her. "No! It can't be! Molly! Kendrick! Sinclair! Radinka!" The spirit fell to her knees. "So long," she wailed. "How can they still keep you like this after so long?"

Portia rushed to her side, but Imogen would not be comforted. There was a sound from the main room downstairs, the sharp *click* of a door shutting. Portia reached out for Imogen's wrist and sank through it. She concentrated on reaching beyond herself, beyond the physical, and caught her companion's hand.

"Come on, we can't help them if we're caught! Let's go!" Portia dragged Imogen down the center aisle between the rows of beds. There was a door at the far side, the dull gleam of its hinges just visible in the dimness. Portia made a dash for it. Inside was a small anteroom containing an overlarge linen closet stacked with towels, sheets, blankets, pillows, and cot mattresses rolled up with coarse twine. She ducked behind a tall stack of them, with Imogen still in tow. She was still crying, but softly now, her ethereal frame wracked with sobs.

No one came into the dormitory. Perhaps those heart-rending screams from the depths of her beloved Imogen's tortured soul had been for Portia's ears alone.

It took a few long minutes until Portia's hammering heart slowed enough for her to catch her breath. "You need to tell me everything you know about what is going on here."

Imogen shook her head. "No." She sputtered and sobbed. "I cannot."

"How do you know those children?"

Her shoulders slumped as if she could still feel the tension in the muscles she once had. "These were my sisters and my brothers, my playmates." Her voice hitched. "They were so good, all of them! I have been gone so long! I had hoped...I had hoped that maybe they'd be dead by now. Free of all this."

"Wait, explain this to me. These children have been here for *fifteen years*? How is that possible?" She paused, remembering. "You came to the Penemue chapter house just after I did. Trust me, I remember. I was in love with you already. We were, what, nine? No, ten years old?"

"*You* were ten."

"Details. So, you were eleven, then?"

Imogen turned away.

"Imogen? Seriously, how old were you when you came to Penemue?"

"Not ten."

Portia glanced toward the door to the dormitory. "And those aren't ordinary children, are they?"

Imogen shook her head. "Not even by our queer standards of 'normal.'"

"What is happening here?"

"There are more rooms beyond here. A washroom and another large dormitory."

"Imogen...."

"We had better check those out. Although I am afraid of what we might find there."

Portia realized she would not get the answer she wanted out of Imogen. "We," she said. "So you are coming with me, then? Think you can handle it?"

The spirit glared hard at her, her dark green eyes glinting. "Of course I can." She stood and drifted through the wall and into the next room.

Portia scrambled to her feet and followed after, emerging into a dank bathroom that reverberated with dripping water. There were toilet stalls to one side and a row of claw-footed bathtubs to the other. The second dormitory was far better lit than the first one had been, and Portia had no problem finding her way to Imogen. She wasn't crying, she wasn't making a sound. Her arms hung still at her sides. She was murmuring, but her words were blurred with horror.

"This was never supposed to happen. It was not supposed to be like this. Not like this."

"Imogen, what wasn't supposed—" The words dried up in Portia's mouth. A floor-to-ceiling curtain hung across the room, and Imogen stood in the opening. Pale blue light shone through her translucent body, but what cast that light was nothing Portia could ever have imagined. Case after case of tall glass enclosed dozens of naked figures. They were tall and lean with elegant features, just like the children, but these were older, just barely adolescent.

Several of them had wings. A few of the wings were fully formed and recognizable, but most were gnarled or stumpy or otherwise tremendously misshapen. Many had gnarled fingers and toes sprouting ragged, talon-like nails. The flesh of some was reddened and lacerated, studded with carbuncles and oozing sores. The limbs of others were withered, legs strapped or even bolted to braces and arms hanging like ruined vines. These creatures behind the glass stood frozen and still, like dolls on display. Their eyes and mouths were wrapped with silk bandages, and a disturbing variety of equipment was attached to their otherwise naked bodies. Small diodes and wires were embedded in their pearly skin.

Portia touched the glass of one of the cases, curiosity battling with disgust. "What is this?"

"Portia, you have to get out of here. I didn't know when we came that *this* was what they were doing! When they find out that you have come here..." Imogen glanced around, nervous and trembling. "Oh God, Portia, I don't want to see you in one of these boxes." Terror was etched deeply into her beautiful face. "You need to get out! Go, Portia. As I love you, please, go! I couldn't bear what they'd do to you!" She hiccupped and doubled over in pain, clutching at her breastbone. "Please! Before they find you!"

"Imogen!"

"Get out of here!" She clenched her eyes shut, gasping and trying to regain composure. "We are here. Against my will. They wish to harm you." Her words were choked out, forced. Her hands remained pressed against her breastbone. She was in obvious pain.

Portia took an uncertain step away. "Why do you know this?"

The ghost shook her head, unable to reply. "Please, just go," she whispered.

"I won't leave you behind."

"Why not?" Imogen hissed. "You did it once before. And I am certainly not in danger of dying this time."

Portia recoiled as if Imogen had struck her. "That's hardly fair. It wasn't like that!" A scuttling noise in the front dormitory caught Portia's attention. She was on the alert at once. "A patrol? Imogen, is that a patrol?"

"We can't fight them, Portia." Her shoulders sagged and her back shook with sobs. "I tried, we all tried. I don't think even you could do it. We have to get out!"

"What is wrong with you?"

"More than I can tell you, I'm afraid. No matter how much I want to."

"This is getting us nowhere. Listen, we're cornered, we are going to need to take a stand."

"No! Portia, you don't understand!"

"And you won't tell me!"

"I *cannot!*" She struck her chest. "Listen to what I am saying to you! I cannot tell you! My words are locked away!"

"We still need to fight what is coming for us!"

Imogen sighed, defeated. She turned toward the sound and vanished. Portia readied her weapon and crouched behind the curtain. She pressed her hip against one of the glass cases, fighting the choke of revulsion from being so close to what floated within it. Whatever it was, it had once been a child. A proud and beautiful descendant of the Nephilim, just like she was. Just like Imogen. She trembled with rage and terror as she nocked her bolt.

The soft shuffling grew louder as the adversary approached through the anteroom and washroom into the second dormitory. Imogen appeared beside her, looking shaken and pale.

"It's bad," she said in a strained voice. It seemed as if the very act of being there and speaking had quite suddenly become extraordinarily draining. She was stroking her sternum.

"How bad?" For a moment Portia wondered if they were speaking about the patrol or something else entirely.

Imogen coughed. "Incubus."

Portia's eyes widened. "An incubus? They have an *incubus* guarding this place?" Her mind shifted immediately to strategy. She was not prepared for this. Common demons were one thing, but a humanoid creature with strength and cunning that could rival her own was a prospect she had not considered. She hoped she had enough bolts. She wished for a gun, specifically one of the new repeating rifles the other Gyony were always on about.

"He seems to have been sent to investigate. He's suspicious."

"No doubt. Now, let's make a plan."

The spirit shook her head, her gaze steeped in regret. "I am not going to be able to help you fight."

"What? Why not? You are a Gyony! You are my partner! And...and...you are my own, my love. Why won't you help me fight?"

"Not won't. *Can't.*"

"This is ridiculous! What could possibly keep you from helping me?"

"Portia, don't. You have no idea, none."

Portia took a deep breath to steady her nerves. "When I am finished dispatching this thing, you will explain to me what's going on here."

Imogen said nothing; she only looked away.

The incubus slunk into the room, its thickly scaled tail scraping the floor in a disturbing susurration that was not unlike the sound of a giant snake. Portia sat back on her heels and brought the crossbow up into position. She would only have one chance to use the element of surprise. She rested her finger on the trigger and waited until the incubus came closer to the split in the curtains. She could barely see the demon's charcoal-black skin from her angle, but there was no mistaking what it was. Its tattered, leathery wings veined with ropy purple vessels. They were folded back against a battered breastplate and a torn, woolen kilt spattered with unseemly stains. Its head swung side to side and the wide nostrils of its flat snout flared as it tested the air for her scent. And then it turned to face her, locking her in a red-filmed gaze that was cold, flat, and nearly reptilian.

Portia aimed the crossbow and whispered a prayer before she squeezed the trigger. But her fingers froze in place, and her arms began to tremble with weakness. The incubus sat back on its massive haunches, tail tip lashing, and closed its eyes. Portia felt her eyelids sink closed as if in answer to the demon's command. When she shook herself free of the drowsiness that rapidly spread through her, she found herself peering through the break in the curtains at a handsome young man. His face was kind and not unlike Emile's, with tawny blond hair and crystalline blue eyes. He gave her a lopsided smile that was sheepish and endearing as he peered at her through the opening of the curtains. The diffused light of the specimen room glowed softly against his broad chest and well-muscled hips. He seemed just about to slip out of the fine tartan kilt he wore. He noticed her scrutiny and he blushed, looking aside before shyly bringing his gaze back to her face. His eyes were wide and dewy, with pupils now so dilated that she would not have been able to say at that moment if they were in fact blue or not.

He came within a few feet of where she sat and settled down into an easy crouch. He leaned in, pushing the curtain aside with his elegant hands. The scent of his skin was magnificent, like warm amber and myrrh. His cheek brushed against hers, and the scruff of his stubble made her shiver.

"Hello there." His voice carried a peculiar lilting accent that took a moment for Portia to place. It was the accent of her home. Not Penemue, but the tiny hamlet where she'd been born, where no one had ever seen an automobile and the old biddies still gathered to gossip at the town well. "You're a lovely one, aren't you?"

She gasped and nodded, eager to have him speak once more, desperate that he touch her.

"I like you, my little dove. Such a sweet and tempting creature, you are." His mouth moved along the curve of her throat until he was pressing kisses into the hollow at its base. She could feel the heat radiating from his flesh as he hovered so very close to her.

In the deep recesses of Portia's mind, a memory began to tickle, and then whisper; it started to prod and finally to scream. Something was *not right.* She struggled to piece together the events of the last few minutes, but found her thoughts as scattered as if some careless hands had been through them and cast them aside as they passed. Urgent kisses traveled up and down her neck, and she felt the tender flesh there pinched between sharp teeth that made her tremble with delight. Distantly, the warnings continued, and only when she moved to put her arms around him did Portia realize she had a crossbow in her lap. She drew back in shock and touched the weapon gingerly. It looked so utterly familiar to her, yet she could not place ever having seen it before. The man kneeling before her reached out to push it aside, but Portia closed her fingers around the stock. She shook her head, not trusting her tongue to words.

He sat back and clucked his tongue. "I suppose a pretty girl should have pretty toys." But he did not want her to have it, that she could tell; the furrow in his brow gave him away. She also realized she had no idea who he was and why she was allowing him to put his lips all over her. She opened her mouth to ask him plainly when half-remembered knowledge tore through the shroud of glamour. She realized that she was kneeling on the floor in a tryst with an incubus.

Portia scuttled backward, gripping the crossbow with a white-knuckled fury. How had he been able to bewitch her? He laughed in a gentle manner that was chillingly out of place as Portia backed up against a glass case. The mute, blind occupant stood slightly slumped and oblivious.

"What's the matter, my darling? Do you not find me beautiful? Do you not desire me?"

"I do not," she whispered, feeling no conviction behind her words. But it was a good beginning, a tiny ledge to grasp to keep from falling back into the abyss of his sensual trickery.

She buried her face into the crook of her elbow, feeling the familiar texture of the cotton canvas. It smelled like her room in the Penemue chapter house, like her soap and faintly like brimstone from her encounter with the fiend only the night before. It seemed so much longer ago than that. The comfort of these mundane scents helped clear her mind. She could understand, in some muddled fashion, that she had indeed been ensorcelled by the incubus. A feat, given her training and the protective charms laid upon her, that should have been impossible.

Her training. It had failed her time and time again. The mistake that allowed a fiend's shriek to turn her hair to white. The avoidable accident that had cost Imogen her life. And now this, canoodling with an incubus. Something was definitely amiss, and it was more than her training. She felt raw and exposed. So easily had the demon been able to dip into her memories without even stirring the surface of her consciousness. It was her training, Portia realized, that had saved her. That could only mean one thing. The charms were gone. And if the charms were gone, that meant Lady Hester....

She shuddered violently and tossed the thought away from her. She had to concentrate on the matter at hand. Her arms weak with yearning, she raised the crossbow. His face was so handsome, yes, so much like Emile. Emile, who had carried Portia away from the garret of her father's house and into a new life. Emile, who had always been so kind and doting. He was the only man for whom Portia had felt any infatuation, and it had been nothing more than a young girl's hero-worship. Now his essence was being used to try to destroy her.

"You chose poorly, you realize," Portia growled, trying to muster her strength beneath a façade of bravado. "Not only the face, but the *gender*."

The young man shrugged and tossed his head to clear

the lock of hair that had fallen perfectly and roguishly across his eyes. "I am limited in certain ways. But come, my dear, let me show you what I am able to do. Every lock needs a key, you know. There is nothing but pleasure in my arms." He held out his hands to her, and for a moment, Portia was swayed. But when she looked into his face, she could see the bloody gleaming of his eyes and the dull shine of row after row of black, pointed teeth between his plump lips.

She braced the crossbow against her belly and pulled the trigger.

The bolt flew free in an instant and the creature froze in his motions, eyes wide, mouth agape. She heard the bolt rend through the curtain and clatter to the floor somewhere across the room. With shaking hands and nearly numb fingers, Portia dug desperately through her bag for a second bolt. But the incubus was sitting very still with a curiously blank expression on his once-handsome face. The high, firm cheekbones were drooping and the shoulders were beginning to slouch. His jaw still hung open, and as he began slowly collapsing to the floor, she could see that she had shot him clean through the mouth and out the back of his neck. Several broken teeth dropped off his tongue and fell to the floor like bits of glass as he toppled forward, trapping Portia between him and the glass specimen case. The heady scent of amber and myrrh was gone; the body instead reeked of sweat and old blood as it quivered and began to thrash in its death throes. Congealed purple-brown blood oozed from the gaping wound and dripped slowly down her shoulder. It burned where it touched her, scalding like hot tea spilled upon her flesh. She writhed and kicked, desperate to roll the demon off of her, but his dead weight had her pinned against the bottom of the case.

She managed to pull one arm free and push the demon's head aside enough to look around her. "Imogen! Imogen, help me!" But there was no one to hear her. Only the dozens of specters of Imogen's childhood friends, unheeding in their glass boxes.

She sighed. Slowly and painfully she started to bring her knees in toward her body. With her shoulders braced against the specimen case, she could manage a good, strong kick if she could get her feet into position. The blood was seeping everywhere, along with other fluids she preferred not to try to identify. The floor was growing slick.

"Portia? Portia, are you all right?"

She froze, wondering if she had imagined the voice. It was not Imogen, of that she was certain. She could see the outline of a woman carrying an electrified lantern. The woman pushed the curtains aside and surveyed the scene.

"Good gracious, child, what have you gotten yourself into this time?" Lady Hester strode forward and knelt beside her. She touched Portia's forehead in a motherly gesture. "Hold on, let me help you."

Between the both of them, they were able to roll the dead incubus off of Portia. Hester offered her hand to help Portia to her feet.

"Careful there." She led the girl away from the pool of thickening blood and offered her a linen handkerchief, which Portia took gratefully. "Do you want to explain what's going on here?"

Portia took a deep breath, unsure of where to begin. "It is a long story. And I truly don't know the half of it. We have to find Imogen." Panic flared, but something gnawed at the edge of her thinking. "Wait, what are you doing here? Are you well?"

"Well enough to come after you. You should have told someone where you were going. Someone else should have come with you and Imogen. This is dangerous business, no place for two young Gyony alone."

Portia's mind reeled wildly between thoughts. She found it nearly impossible to think of more than one simple thing at a time. "Did you see Imogen when you arrived, Lady Hester? Can you sense her here?"

Hester tilted her head as if listening. "Nothing."

Portia sighed, trying to clear the dust that seemed to be settling all over her words. "Imogen could explain this better. She used to live here, with these...children. I don't know what's happening here, but something is very wrong."

"Wrong? Like what?"

"Besides the children kept in comas in their beds and the adolescents in glass specimen cases?" Her voice arced with fear.

"Besides that, yes." Lady Hester was imperturbable as always.

Portia collected herself. "My transmitter. It started *talking* to me."

"It did?" Hester raised an eyebrow. "What did you hear?"

"A prayer, or at least some incantation. I don't know what it was." Portia ran her hands through her hair. The kerchief was gone, somewhere in the congealed mess of blood. She glanced back and did not see it right off, but realized her well-loved Gladstone bag was still there, soaking up a disturbing amount of liquid.

"What did it sound like?" Hester pressed her, and Portia forced her mind back on track.

"Some of it I understood, but a lot of it was foreign, another language. I'm sorry I can't be more helpful."

"It's fine. I think I have an idea about this."

"You do? Wonderful. I was starting to feel like I was in over my head here."

Lady Hester chuckled and put her arm around Portia's shoulders. They began walking toward the door. "Oh no, Portia, you are just where you are supposed to be. Everything is just fine."

"That's good." Portia relaxed against her body, feeling the stress and fear drain out of her. She leaned her head onto Lady Hester's shoulder and the woman pressed a kiss into her silvery, blood-splattered hair. She felt sheepish for needing to be rescued, especially since she was less than a year from her age of majority and ought to be entirely self-sufficient, but it still felt so good to be caressed and coddled. To be petted and loved like her mother had never petted or loved her. She skipped a step. Her mother had never been affectionate to her in all her memory. And she had always wished in her deepest heart of hearts for Lady Hester to take that place in her life. She imagined grandiose scenarios wherein Hester played the part of Portia's mother and kissed her elbows when they got scraped and cheered at piano recitals and taught her how to pour the perfect cup of tea. Those fantasies always ended with warm embraces and tender words. And they were all nothing but fantasies. Lady Hester was a kind woman, a devoted Edulica who deeply loved all the children in her care, but she was never one for physical intimacies of any sort. And here she was with Portia cuddled close by, fawning over her.

"I am so very glad to see that you are well again, Lady Hester."

"Portia, my heart, you know that nothing could ever keep me from you. Of all the children, you have always been the most dear to my heart, my secret favorite."

And her soul sang with joy to hear it, although her heart sank at the stunning cold truth. Rarely did an incubus hunt alone. His mate was always nearby. And succubi were far more cunning in their seductions. The satchel full of charms and weapons was in the other room now, most likely stuck fast to the floorboards with gore. Portia had nothing but her wits and whatever protections might still be upon her. But seeing this perfect form of Lady Hester beside her, she knew those blessings could no longer be relied upon. The steadfast matron of the chapter house of Penemue was dead. She had to be, or at least completely lost to the waking world in a coma.

"Are we going to alert the Primacy about this?" Portia indicated the rows and rows of narrow beds and their still and silent occupants. She played along, stalling until she could formulate a plan. But thinking was so difficult, everything in her head was moving so slowly and her shoulder ached like mad where the demon's blood had burned her.

"Of course." Lady Hester nodded as she gazed around

her at the sleeping children. "They will be made aware as soon as possible. This cannot continue."

"Oh, good. Imogen will be so glad to hear." The relief surprised her. As if this creature would really help put an end to the barbaric experimentation.

"Besides," Lady Hester stopped and held Portia out at arm's length. "We won't be needing them anymore, now that we have you."

"You...what?"

Lady Hester snatched the Saint Christopher medallion from around Portia's neck, snapping the slender chain with a little spark of light. She then cupped Portia's face and kissed her. The kiss was the single most penetrating and ravaging thing she had ever experienced. What began as a simple, human tongue swelled into a thick and nimble appendage that seemed to have a mind of its own. It forced itself down her throat, growing longer and more slender the deeper it burrowed until she felt a sharp stab of pain behind her breastbone. The last thing Portia saw was Lady Hester's face close against hers, eyes rolled back in concentration, her jaw unnaturally unhinged. The corners of her mouth were stretched taut and the skin was pushed up and puckered around her elegant nose. Portia hated her for taking the face of the woman who had been the only mother she'd ever really known. She raked her fingers against Lady Hester's throat and chest, but her strength faded quickly, and soon she had no more will to fight. As the succubus drank from her heart's blood, Portia's world went dark.

4

Shadow shapes played across Portia's closed eyelids, and from somewhere distant she could hear the laughter of children. But it was not a comforting sound; it was aching and haunting, discordant. Portia struggled to shake free of sleep, but it held her tightly. Slowly the silhouettes blurred into the encroaching dimness and she briefly realized that it was night once more. The dreams came and went, leaving tears in their wake.

In one dream, Imogen was standing over her with a bowl of cool water, bathing her hurt shoulder and rubbing in some kind of salve. She wanted so much to speak to her, to pull her close and just kiss her. The memory of Imogen's flesh beneath her lips flared fresh and painful, choking her with nostalgia. She tried to speak, if only to overcome her encompassing weakness long enough to just say her name.

"Mmmm-nnnnnn," was all she could muster. It exhausted her, and she could feel the sweat gathering at the back of her neck.

The dream Imogen tilted her head, and sunlight gleamed in her red hair. She leaned close, letting those brilliant sunset curls fall over Portia's face. She kissed her with such delicate and restrained passion, gliding her tongue just beneath Portia's parched lips. She tasted, as she always had, of vanilla and strawberries. Portia struggled to lift her arms and wrap them around her beloved, but they would not respond to her commands. Her left hand twitched, brushing against Imogen's smooth hip. Portia reveled in that tiny touch as exhaustion swelled and drove the dream away into darkness as she slept deeply again.

"**Lamia was quite overzealous,**" spoke a female voice in a heady drawl. "The girl will be of no use to us dead."

"She will live," answered another, so familiar. "She is stronger than you think. And far more stubborn, too."

"Perfect," the woman almost purred. "This is just the start for her."

Portia rose slowly into wakefulness, although her body remained thick and sluggish. Both voices, she realized, she had heard before. The woman's was the same velvety tone that had come over the transmitter. And the other sounded so much like Imogen, but it could not be. Imogen no longer had a voice.

They moved away and began to murmur too softly to be heard. The door opened and someone else entered the room.

"After all this planning! I cannot believe you almost killed her! Idiots! Amateurs!" Portia could hear the inflated bombast covering his feeling of inadequacy, his fear of failure. The rushed thump of his footfalls told the same story. And as always, he covered his weakness with a ferocious show of temper. Portia knew this bit of playacting all too well; she had been an audience to it for years. Nigel had forever been a grasping, conniving coward who rarely lifted a finger to do for himself, preferring to bully the rest of his companions and playmates into doing the work instead, and now he was somehow wrapped up this terrible endeavor. Portia was not surprised.

The voices continued, their hushed tones rising and piling on top of one another. The someone who sounded like Imogen came to stand at the foot of the bed, defiance clear in her voice though her words fell just out of Portia's hearing. But her stand was cut short. The slap resounded louder than the shouts and the red-haloed shadow doubled over and sank out of Portia's limited sight.

"Damn it, Imogen!" Nigel could be clearly heard, he always made sure of that, especially when he was angry. A scuffle followed and another heavy hit that made Portia want to leap from the bed to defend her lover, but Nigel left the room and, from the sound of it, dragged Imogen out with him. The door slammed and the air was still. She could not wrap her mind around what was happening. Did she truly hear Nigel strike Imogen? Did that mean the Imogen was real and solid enough to be struck? And what was she doing here with these people? Portia struggled for a moment, but felt a cool hand on her wrist.

"Hush, now. You're going to need your rest, little silver-hair. Tomorrow is going to be quite a big day for you." The hazy image of the woman bent over a low table and came back holding something in her hand. Portia saw the light glint off of a long needle and a thick cylinder of glass. She felt a pinch in the crook of her elbow and the pressure of fluid being administered. It was cold, so very cold, and it sank into her bones, dragging her downward into what felt like the bottom of the ocean. She cried out, or at least thought she did, but the woman left the room without a single glance back. Portia fumbled in her mind for a prayer, an incantation, anything that might save her.

"Dymphna, Saint and Savioress of the mentally ill, clear my eyes and let me see, free me from these danger-ous illusions and let me wake with True Sight! Saint Dym-phna, I call you to my side!"

But no one came. Portia tumbled into unconsciousness and her words echoed in the tight confines of her own mind; she had not the strength to utter one sound.

Portia's head was being lifted and lowered. She stirred and reached up to touch her face. A strip of silk bandage was smoothed over her eyes. She bucked and pushed away the hands that ministered to her. Although her body felt list-less and hesitant, it was obeying her commands. She clawed the bandage from her eyes and opened them boldly.

"You'll explain yourself!" She glared at the figure as if she could truly see.

"Oh, Portia."

"Imogen?" The sunlight was dazzling, but she could make out a head of rich red hair. "Imogen, what's going on?"

She sighed and sat on the edge of the narrow bed. She twined her long fingers into Portia's silver hair. "There is not enough time to explain."

Portia grabbed Imogen's fingers. "How is this possible? This?" She gripped them, feeling the delicate bones within and watching Imogen wince.

"I am still dead, Portia. This is my body and it houses my soul, but it is an unnatural marriage."

"Aldias?"

Imogen nodded. "This has been long in the planning, my love. Nigel has just sped things up. And I am sorry to have ever been a part of it, regardless that it was against my will. You must understand that I had no choice."

Portia sputtered, crushed between fury and terror. "No *choice*? In what? In luring me to my death? Or in loving me?"

"We have very little time, and I have no patience for histrionics right now. You shall not die. And I have always loved you." She reached out for Portia's hand, but Portia jerked it away. "Portia, please."

"*Please*? Please, what?" Portia pulled away, pressing her back up against the narrow wrought-iron headboard. "Accept that my entire life has been a *lie*?"

Imogen sighed. "It was a well-laid plan made long ago. The Lady Analise, as ambitious and cruel as she is beautiful, has spent her entire life hunting for us. She calls us the Pure Children. We are her Holy Grail. It will be through us and our *Bene 'elim* blood that she can achieve her end."

"And what is that?"

Imogen glanced about furtively and leaned close to whisper into Portia's ear. "She seeks to destroy the Primacy and bring about the end of the Grigori."

"*What*? Why?"

"That she may remake it according to her own designs. Her ambitions were always larger than her abilities, even after she found us out. We were studied, tested, and grouped according to our strength. And that is as far as it went for many years."

"What was she looking for?"

"We never knew. Until Nigel came."

Portia saw the rows of beds and the chamber full of glass cases. She shuddered. "The experiments?"

Imogen nodded. "Lady Analise began bringing him up from Penemue when he was but eight years old. It was the year you came to the chapter house. They knew about you early on and they were brimming with plans. The rituals and tests on the others, they have been all in preparation for your arrival."

Portia gagged. "You can't be serious! What do they want with *me*?"

"I am not entirely certain. All I know is that fifteen years ago, I was specifically selected to be sent to you. They wanted me to ingratiate myself unto you, to spy on you, to lure you here when they felt the time was right."

Portia's mouth narrowed into a thin line and she kept her tone even. "So, it *was* a lie, after all."

"No, Portia! Of all us here in this convent, our secluded paradise, I was chosen to be banished, for reasons I will never understand. I was the one torn away from the only home I had ever known and sent away. But I had never been so glad to have fallen from grace. What I found with you, my love, was worth the pain, the suffering, the long lonely nights I spent cut off from my brothers and sisters and our sweet, gentle guardians. I had no idea what horrible fate had befallen them in my lengthy absence, that they would still be here...and in that condition after all these years..." She shuddered and scooped up Portia's hands in her own. "It is no lie that I love you. Had the choice been laid before me once more, knowing what I do now, I would say yes. A thousand times over."

Portia was not wholly convinced, but the sensation of Imogen's fingers clasped around her own, feeling her lover's leaping pulse and agitated breath, was intoxicating. "So, then, tell me. Your death? Was that part of this grand scheme?"

She shook her head. "No. At least I don't think so. When I met my untimely death, it was unexpected, by me and by the others. I thought that maybe then I was free. And I had never loved you more for that. I imagined that somehow you knew and you were releasing me. But Nigel was quick and he was clever. He corralled my soul before it fled and fettered me to the realm of the living. And so, I have carried on in my task, unwillingly. But truly, and you must believe this, my love for you has and always will be real, Portia." Imogen unbuttoned the high-collared blouse she wore and laid her chest bare. An arcane symbol was carved deeply through her flesh and into her breast-bone. Portia could see that new blood glimmered atop an old scar. "I can give you no more assurance than this. This is how I am bound. To undo it, all you must do is disrupt this sign. Cut with your fingernails if you need to."

"Why are you telling me this?"

"Because it is a knowledge you may need. This body was once mine, but not anymore. The Aldias pull my strings now. I have as much free will as any clockwork doll. There is no choice in my bones, although my tongue has more freedom than it once had. I know not why, but only that it somehow serves Nigel's purpose that I am able to speak freely to you."

"This is all Nigel's doing?"

"He plays the master, yes."

"Then I am really going to enjoy his slow, agonizing death at my hands."

"Portia, but this runs deeper than his involvement. It was Lady Analise's brainchild, but she was hardly alone. Perhaps it is the work of all of the Aldias, I don't know."

"Than I shall just have to kill her, too. It's as simple as that."

Imogen stifled a peccant snicker. "You are a Gyony through and through, my love."

Portia was not to be deterred. "But why Lady Hester? Her blood is on their hands. Tell me, don't they deserve a vicious demise for that? Why did she have to die? What was her role in all of this?"

Imogen looked down at her hands, picking at some minute bit of lint on her skirt. "Because Lady Hester knew what I was and why I was there."

Portia straightened, her still-drugged muscles protesting. "She *knew*?" Snippets of half-remembered conversations clicked together like cogs and sprockets. "The other night, after the fiend. She asked if you had been with me. She made a note of it in her papers."

"And then Nigel came to your room, and the next night you were summoned here. The Aldias keep tabs on *everything*."

Portia nodded. "From what I gather, Lady Hester had written a letter to the Primacy that was to be sent in the morning by special courier. Someone must have put a stop to it."

"Do you mean Nigel? At his bidding, I am certain, but not at his doing." Imogen smirked. "Do you really think Nigel would dirty his own hands?"

Portia laughed despite herself. "No, not him, that spoiled princeling."

"Some things will never change." Imogen sighed.

For a moment, the clock had been turned back many years, the two of them in one of their rooms whispering and laughing and gossiping long into the night. But the cold reality was all too close and it only took a moment for the shared mirth to fade away again, replaced by suspicion, anger, and fear.

"Imogen," Portia began.

The girl shook her head. "Not now. I have dallied here overlong, and Nigel and Lady Analise will be suspicious." She cocked her head to one side. "I hear her assistant coming now. I must bandage you before Katriel takes you, so your eyes do not sit open and dry out. And I must wrap your mouth for the same reason. Please, do not fight me."

Portia lay back down, still holding onto her lover's hand, unwilling to let the full magnitude of what Imogen had told her sink into her heart. "They've always owned you. The entire time I have known you, you were theirs."

Imogen chose her words carefully. "My body, but never my heart," she said. "Before that, I played in these gardens and ran through these courtyards under the golden sun as free as any plain human child, never knowing

I was something else. In this pure, protected place we never comprehended that we did not age as ordinary children do. And when Analise Aldias came here, nearly two hundred years ago, she was cunning and sincere. The poor nuns believed her when she said she was a victim of the Grigori Primacy, here to search for her stolen child. They had no love for the Grigori, for their methods of removing children from their homes to be raised in chapter houses all across the countryside. Her tears seemed so honest. And then she brought the others with her. I looked through their faces to see if I recognized my mother or my father. We all did. As much as we loved the sweet sisters, we longed to know what our own families were like and if they wanted us back. And they did want us, the children born of a truer Nephilim bloodline. The Pure Children, they called us, *Bene 'elim*, they called us. The ordinary Grigori children had failed them, they said. They needed us to help them. We were the only ones that could."

"Yes, *Bene 'elim*. That is what the woman said..." Portia reached for the transmitter in her pocket out of habit but realized her beloved duster was gone, and she wore only a simple linen shift that was too tight around the hips. "Was that Lady Analise we heard?"

Imogen nodded. "Now lie still, Katriel's coming." She quickly bound Portia's eyes. "Portia, my love, you shall not die." Before Imogen wrapped Portia's mouth, she kissed her. "I love you."

The silk smothered Portia's reply as Imogen swaddled her lips firmly shut.

The wrapping over Portia's eyes was so snug that she could not open them at all. She desperately looked back and forth, sensing only shadows from behind her closed eyelids and layers of pale bandages. Not only was her mouth gagged, but bandages looped under her chin like a wimple kept her jaws shut as well. The only sounds she could make were hums and whimpers.

She had been placed in a chair, her arms and legs buckled securely to it with leather straps. The chair was then wheeled along a corridor and into a small, creaking room. Axle grease and exhaust fumes pervaded the air. Portia guessed, and rightly so, that she was in an elevator. Downward she sank until her companion pulled the lever that brought the elevator to a halt, and then the doors clattered open.

She knew her destination without having to see. The soft blue light of the specimen room was recognizable even through the yards of silk covering her closed eyes. Footfalls and the squeak of her wheelchair bounced back off of the glass cases to either side. She was surprised that they passed them completely. In what must have been the very far end of the room, she heard a curtain being withdrawn. Efficient hands unbuckled her from the chair and lifted her onto a metal table. Portia could not keep from trembling.

"Why are you frightened, my little silver-haired angel?" The woman asked the question as if she expected an answer. It was a familiar voice, with melodious vowels and a lilting quality to her words. Lady Analise.

Portia made a token attempt at a reply that she knew sounded like nothing at all. The woman laughed, and it

was not comforting. "I will tell you now, you poor, ignorant child, that I am not going to kill you. In fact, I cannot
kill you, did you know that? It is not in my power or ability. You will indeed live to see this through." She chuckled again, "Of course, you might *wish* you were dead, but
live you shall." She paced with measured steps around the
table. Portia began to count them. "I am willing to bet
that you do not even know what you are, do you? You
have no idea. In fact, I don't even think the Edulica or
Gyony really know what you are, although they really
should. I mean, that is their job, isn't it?"

Analise paused again, as if awaiting an answer. She
continued her pacing, her voice rising in pitch. "They
should have looked closer at you and taken better care of
you! But obviously they couldn't be bothered, so by rights
they had no claim to you, really. Witless Hester Edulica
never even bothered to question your mother, did you
know that? She took your mother's dolt of a husband at
his word. Your mother's *husband*, I chose that word specifically, do you understand? He was not your father." It
took fifteen steps for her to make the circuit around the
table. "I made sure to speak to the *both* of them directly
after Nigel told us about your hair. Because I am not an
idiot."

"Mmmm hrrrrrr?" *My hair? What has that to do with
anything?*

"Yes, darling." Her fingers were icy cold against
Portia's forehead. "Once you were old enough that it began to turn, oh, it was a simple matter of sweeping a few
memories under the proverbial rug, keeping you from the
knowledge of it. Clever, don't you think? Goodness, what

did we have that memory replaced with? Oh, yes, a fiend's death wail. Yes, that certainly can turn the hair white, even in our kind. White, but not *silver*. A trivial detail, easily overlooked. And given your sense of modesty and your hurt pride, thanks to Nigel, we made certain not enough people saw it to even begin a debate about its color. Of course Hester, the damn harpy, was curious. But she was dealt with." She stroked Portia's hair, careful not to dislodge the wrappings. "Now, child, why is this important? Are you curious?"

When she paused in her touch and her words, Portia hurried to nod and answer, "Mmmm-hmmm."

"Oh, good! Curiosity is powerful, you know. Powerful enough to overcome many things: fear, isolation, pain. It is a ripe reward at the end of a long journey." Portia felt the pinch of a needle in her arm and the cold drag of the strong sedative. "Part of that journey is earning that reward, being patient enough to see things through to their inevitable conclusion."

There were others in the room; she could hear them breathing and shuffling their feet now and again. They wheeled something near to the table, something that rattled quietly of metal on metal.

"Lady Analise, we are ready to begin when you are." The voice came from somewhere to the left, or so Portia thought; the sedatives were quickly numbing her remaining senses. The voice was low and smooth, but she could not determine if it was the voice of a man or a woman.

"Thank you, Katriel. Let us begin with the scissors." With her failing hearing, Portia heard Lady Analise snip a lock of hair from near her ear. "And now, if you could be so kind as to hand me the scalpel?"

—5—

She was upright, that much was certain. It was a strange sensation to be standing when she felt otherwise so relaxed. Vaguely aware of a pale, bluish light all around her, Portia realized that she must have been put in one of the glass cases. She knew that there were close to two dozen of them in the room along with her, yet she felt entirely isolated. Her toes flexed and stretched and gave Portia a start. A thigh muscle twitched in response, and her body weight shifted of its own accord. The disturbing sensation confirmed that her mind was far removed from the workings of her body. She attempted to reach up and push back the bandages over her eyes, but her hands would not so much as twitch. In fact, her eyes did not even bother to answer her commands. They looked neither left nor right and did not even try to blink. She floated, fully conscious and aware, in a useless mannequin.

Portia began to cry, but the sounds echoed only through the confines of her mind.

When the attendant came for her, she had no idea how long she'd been standing in her glass case among all the others, blind, mute, paralyzed, and bathed in blue light that was the very color of a perfect summer sky.

The hands that reached into her little glassed-in world were gentle when they removed her, but she was far gone from her own skin. There was a distant tug and pinch as each diode gave way.

The same able hands laid her down and rolled her away on a squeaky wheeled gurney. They turned right, out of the room and along what felt like an open corridor. The rickety elevator felt almost familiar now, something she knew, something she recognized. Down it took her. The disorientation made Portia dizzy, but the deadly calm of her body truly distressed her. Portia's mind panicked, racing and sputtering. She wanted to scream and tear at her hair, and she felt frightened enough to kick and thrash, but her flesh and bones lay still and unperturbed.

The scent tipped her off. Heady beeswax candles and balsamic, spicy incense overlaid the earlier smell of lye and the nearly indecipherable tang of blood. It set her senses roiling like a storm surge in the vast sea inside her head. The chapel.

Dread reverberated through her body and her muscles seized. She flexed her fingers, but too soon they drifted away from her once more. A moan of frustration escaped her and someone tapped her mouth gently.

"Shhhh."

The straps around her were released and her body drank in a deep breath of its own accord. Hands brought her up from the gurney and put her onto bare wood. Her feet and arms dangled off the sides of the altar. Portia had never felt so exposed in her life.

And then someone removed the silk bandages from her face.

She gazed up into the small steeple of the chapel. Something was suspended there, dangling from a set of copper chains. It looked like a reliquary, but Portia could not force her eyes to focus onto it. She was aware of people moving around her, but could not turn her head to look.

"Don't you worry," said that same genderless voice she had heard before. "She's got it right this time, and you are like none other."

A face leaned over her, as androgynous as the voice. Silver hair curled around sharply angled green eyes and beautifully planed cheekbones.

"Hhhhhuurrrrryuuu?" It was a battle to speak, to force her tongue to obey the command that came so clearly into her mind.

"Are you asking me who I am? Ah, you are such the strong one. I am called Katriel." Katriel produced an ivory comb and showed it to Portia before beginning to comb out her pale hair. "So strong and so beautiful. There is no small wonder why Imogen loves you so much."

"Immmmennnn?"

"Yes, Imogen. Unfortunately, she could not be here to see this. The Lady Analise does not trust her not to interfere, sadly. So Master Nigel is keeping care of her."

Portia could only manage to vocalize a whimper of the torrent of anger, fear, and fierce protectiveness of Imogen.

"There now, Master Nigel means only the best." Katriel nodded emphatically. "He is a true gentleman."

A true gentleman who murdered our foster mother! You cannot leave him alone with Imogen!

"Ah, my Lady." Katriel turned Portia's head with gentle hands.

The door that led in from the sacristy opened, and for the first time Portia saw her captor. Lady Analise was tall and willowy and might have been beautiful once, but her honey-gold hair was pulled back into a severe bun that flattened the features of her face. Her eyes were as grey as the streaks in her hair, and she did not smile. Portia recognized the sound of her clipped steps at once. They were at such odds with the musical lilt of her voice.

"Katriel, will you stop wasting time? The apex of the new moon is but minutes away. If you cause us to miss this chance, I'll be quite cross with you. Now, get to work!"

"Yes, m'lady." The androgynous assistant vanished from Portia's view and began laying out instruments beyond the edges of her sight.

Analise came to stand before Portia, regarding her with eyes as cold as steel. Over her crisp brown taffeta gown, she tied the sash of a stiff white apron, the heavy and gore-proof kind that butchers wore.

"Poor, ignorant child. You have lived your whole life not knowing who and what you were, haven't you? Such a pity. Had we not recognized Nigel's exceptional prowess, he might have languished for years as an ordinary little mongrel Grigori thug, just like you. House Gyony." She rolled her eyes. "Useless ruffians. They had you by all honest rights and never knew what you were, can you believe it? One of the few living Nephilim born directly of a union between celestial and mortal, and able to bear the weight of the power of an angel's soul. All those years, and no one guessed at what you were." She stroked

Portia's silver hair, letting it slide through narrow fingers tipped with long, claw-shaped nails painted a poisonous red. "But not any longer, no. I know what you are, my dear girl, and I am going to see to it that you fulfill the destiny for which you were born."

Katriel took hold of first each wrist and then each ankle and buckled them tightly into a leather strap before shackling all four of Portia's limbs to the altar. Then, with exquisite care, the androgyne took a pair of sewing shears and cut away the shift Portia wore, leaving her trembling and entirely exposed. Katriel tilted her head into position, resting it on a mealy pillow that smelled of myrrh and amber and sulphur. Portia gazed wide-eyed up into the cupola, unable to blink or look anywhere but at the reliquary that hung ominously above her, so gleaming and clean amongst the tattered sheets of cobwebs. An involuntary shudder passed through her, rattling the chains that snaked down off the altar to thick eyebolts in the floor. A web of copper wires connected to the reliquary, fanned out from it, suspended by tiny steel hooks set into the joists of the cupola before each strand twisted into a single bunch and attached to the contact point of an engine. The simple turbine machine sat lashed inelegantly to a tea cart someone had wheeled into the chapel. Two figures worked the crank handle on the back side of the contraption, bobbing up and down in opposition as the turbine began to hum.

All around the altar, ribbons of smoke curled up from incense braziers. A low chanting chorus began as, one by one, the beeswax pillar candles were snuffed out to be replaced by oily, guttering flames of small votives held in earthenware cups. The grimy black smoke stank like burnt hair.

The chanting increased in volume and urgency, reverberating through the chapel. *"Bene 'elim! We claim our birthright! As Bene 'elim, we sing praises to the Most High! Amen! Amen! Amen!"* The voices floated in the dark, buoyed by those leaping orange flames.

Analise had donned a pair of round glass goggles bound in brass frames. In them, Portia could see her own face, pale and impassive with pupils so wide in unblinking eyes that she would not have known their color. She could also see the scalpel that Analise raised.

She felt the sensation of her flesh being parted from a great distance. There was no pain, only the cold rush of air against warm blood and the scrape of the blade's tip against her breastbone. With a face blank of emotion, Analise cleaved through skin and muscle, exposing Portia's ribs and beating heart. She then took a gold stylus and scraped some sigil into the stark white sternum. Next came a handful of herbs and ashes that landed across Portia's body like some mockery of snow printed in negative, black flecks across pale bone.

Lady Analise stepped away and looked up into the cupola. The chanting around them grew louder and more intense. The wires became incandescent as the turbine's hum grew stronger and higher in pitch. Something in the reliquary gleamed with a fitful reddish light, part electrical surge, part something else. Analise cleared her throat, and the chanting faded into silence but the turbine continued to sing. She raised her voice along with it, her notes rising up into the rafters of the chapel that was now filled with a dusky glow.

"Can the wings of the winds understand your voices of wonder, O you, the second of the first, whom the burning flames have framed within the depth of my Laws; whom I have prepared as Cups for a Wedding, or as the flowers in their beauty for the Chamber of Righteousness?" The words were in a strange dialect, the lost language of Enoch. She had never heard it spoken before. "Stronger are your feet than the barren stone, and mightier are your voices than the manifold winds. For you are become a building such as is not, but in the mind of the All Powerful. Arise, sayeth the First; move therefore unto His servants; show yourselves in power; and make me a strong Seething; for I am of Him that liveth for ever."

Somewhere a bell chimed several times.

"Come, come into this child of the Most High. Sever your ties to the celestial plane and cleave to her half-soul, making it whole. I claim my birthright to call upon you, I bind you with my words and with my blood, I sacrifice to you the very flesh of your children."

Analise raised one of the small votive candles and held it aloft in her left hand. Her right hand bled from a cut across her palm and she let several drops of her garnet blood splash into the candle's flame.

"O you, the sons of fury, the daughters of the lust, vexing all creatures of the earth with age, behold the Voice of God, the promise of Him, which is called amongst you Fury or Extreme Justice. Move and show your selves; open the Mysteries of your creation; be friendly unto me, for I am the servant of the same your God, the true worshipper of the Highest!" She moved again from Portia's view as the blood-soaked smoke wafted around the reliquary. "I command you! I command you! I command you!"

The lurid glow around the reliquary exploded into a starburst of flame and sparks. Portia could not blink or look away as tears filled her eyes to cool them. The corona elongated into a single thick pillar of fire that struck her breastbone. Her spine stiffened and her arms and legs made every attempt to rend themselves from her body. The otherworldly scream reverberating through the chapel was issuing from her own throat, she realized. The distance and numbness that had been separating her mind from her flesh stretched and snapped in an instant. Every cell was afire and shrieking. Pressure mounted within her, crushing the breath from her painfully exposed lungs. Portia could tilt her head just enough to see her skin begin to smolder like embers. As the last tongues of flame penetrated her sternum, she saw the spectral image of a person hovering above her. Great golden wings stretched across the whole of her field of vision. Eyes as deep and dark as the eternity of night sky regarded her with sorrow, confusion, and fear. Its mouth stretched wide in a rictus of pain, and it would have howled as mightily as the winter wind if it had the power to scream.

Analise's slender, long-nailed hand shot out between them, a golden seal clenched in her fist. She pressed it into the chest of the spirit with a flash of white light. The form of a sigil appeared there, and it drew ever nearer to the matching one carved into Portia's breastbone. The celestial being fought valiantly, but the moment the two signs touched, an eruption of light obliterated the sight of everything around Portia. The roar of the spirit shook her bones to the marrow. The swinging reliquary above her head shattered, sending bits of glass and melted copper and what looked like charred bone raining down onto the altar and the hardwood floor.

And then all was silent.

Portia closed her eyes and drew a shaking breath. Tremors raced through her body as she tugged on the restraints. The empty, ruined reliquary swung in the cupola, dragging sparking wires in its wake. Nothing else moved. The room swam in blackness, but Portia could see perfectly. The two figures who had turned the turbine crank were seated in the pew beside the tea cart, panting from exertion. Katriel stood beside a metal tray full of medical implements. Portia saw his true form easily in the small, battered body he currently wore. Although the *elohim* were, in essence, genderless, they did sway to one side or the other, masculine or feminine, and Katriel had been a being of near-divinity once. Not born, but made. A heavenly creature lured or dragged from his place in the heavens, now forced to serve his earth-bound cousins, the Nephilim of the Grigori. Somewhere in her memory, she thought she remembered his face from long ago, but the thought distorted then vanished like ripples on the miller's pond back in Penemue.

She smiled, however, and licked her parched lips. In a voice that was hers, yet not her own, she said to the androgynous angel beside her, "Greetings, Brother."

Katriel's nod was curt. "Greetings, Sister."

His voice was carefully bland as he came to the edge of the altar with Analise at his heels. His face was impassive, but hers was ecstatic. "Please forgive me," he whispered as he handed the lady a copper-bound hypodermic needle.

Portia nodded and noticed the gaping wound that was her chest. She felt neither pain nor panic as Katriel held her shoulders firmly and Analise injected unconsciousness into her arm once more.

6

The corridor was long and narrow and oppressively dark. Shadows seemed almost tangible as they writhed around Portia in a frightening, lurching sort of dance. What little light there was seemed to emanate softly from her body. She held up a hand and saw that indeed her flesh glowed gently with a pale, golden light. She tried in vain to pierce the heavy dark that clouded the corridor in either direction.

"Which way do I go?" Her voice reverberated away from her, became lost in the shadows, and returned to her ears in a feeble, thready echo. *Go? Go? Go? Go? Go?*

"Fine! If you're not going to help me—"

Help me! Help me! Help me! Help me! Help me!

Portia took a step away to the left, thinking that she would explore one side of the hallway to its end and then double back. She had nothing with which to mark her passage, so she plucked a few of her own silver hairs, tied them into a knot, and hung the glimmering bundle on a tiny outcropping of stone or plaster or whatever it was that the corridor was made from. The hair hung there, twisting a little, looking like a bit of broken spider's web. Satisfied, she set off into the black ahead of her.

After a few yards, Portia had a most disturbing sense of

having chosen the wrong path. She could not place the sensation, only that something was happening behind her and she needed to investigate. Turning on her heel, she made a few quick strides back, only to find the passage blocked by an imposing and moldering brick wall. At the very corner where the wall met the passageway hung her little knot of hair. It hung perfectly still now, mocking the fact that moments before there had been no wall there.

"What's going on?"

Portia expected the echo, but not this one. *Go! Go! Go! Go! Go!* thundered down on her from behind the old bricks. She bolted.

She ran, on and on down the empty corridor. It had no crossings and no curves. It sloped neither up nor down. There were no decorations of any kind along the endless walls; it was simply an eternity of grey stone that appeared and vanished in the dark. And somehow, Portia knew that if she turned back, she would encounter that mildewed brick wall just a few yards behind her and inches away would hang that damned little knot of hair. But on she ran, terror fueling her legs and echoing in the muffled slap of her bare feet on the stone floor.

She ran until her lungs ached and her heart pounded every sensible thought out of her head, but on and on the corridor stretched. She stumbled to a halt and panted until she caught her breath. And as if she needed such assurances, she summoned her courage, turned, and calmly walked back the way she'd come.

Of course the wall was there. Just a few feet behind her, as if she had been running in place. The little knot of hair hung still as a windless summer day. Turning her back on the unavoidable brick, she walked away as serenely as she could manage.

"What am I doing here?" she challenged her echo.

Here? Here? Here?

"Yes. Why is that wall perpetually behind me?"

Here...Behind...Here...Behind...

"Behind. You are behind me? Who are you?"

You. You. You. You.

"You are not me!"

Not me! You? Not me! You?

"This is ridiculous! What am I doing here? What is the meaning of this?"

Meaning! Meaning! Meaning! You! You! You! The eerie reflection of her own voice faded only for a moment before it returned and urged her once more, *Go!*

But Portia was too tired to run. She trudged on ahead, every now and again sensing the looming presence of the wall behind her, making it seem as if she had not moved more than a few inches in what seemed like hours.

"Perhaps I am not asking the right questions."

Perhaps...questions. Perhaps...questions.

"You told me to go. Go where?"

Where? Where? Where?

"Yes! Where? This corridor has no end!"

End! End! End! Here...behind. Here...behind.

She turned back toward the wall. It was the end of the corridor. Behind her, the passage continued into infinity with no intersections, no slope, and no turns. But before her was the wall, grey-green lichen and moss growing across its surface. She touched it, and it felt damp, brittle, weak.

"Is this correct?"

Correct...Correct...Correct...

"You are here? Behind the wall?"

Here...Behind the wall...Here...Behind the wall...

"How can I know if you are just repeating everything back to me?"

Repeating everything? Repeating everything?

"Are you just repeating everything I say back to me?"

No.

Portia stepped back. "Well, all right, then. What do I do now?"

Now...Now...Now...

She ran her fingers along the grainy mortar between the bricks. She could feel a fissure running through the wall from nearly as high as she was able to reach down to the floor. A parallel one ran down a few feet away.

"Do I push?"

Push! Push! Push!

She gave an experimental press of her hands against the brickwork. Some of the mortar crumbled away, but nothing else happened.

"How hard?"

Hard! Hard! Hard! Push hard! Push hard! Push hard!

Portia leaned into the wall and dug her bare toes into the floor as much as she could. At first they scrambled for purchase, but finally her foot caught the edge of a stone and she used it to lever her shoulders into the wall. It creaked a little and groaned as old bricks were wont to do, but it did not budge.

"I can't do it," she panted.

Do it! Do it! Do it! The echo was louder now, almost a

voice unto itself. *Push hard! Push hard!*

"I haven't the strength."

Strength! Strength! Strength!

"I will get in there, so help me, if to do nothing more than to tell you to *shut the hell up!*"

The echo said nothing in reply.

Portia blew out her breath and drew in another, and another, feeling as if her lungs would break open. She threw her shoulder against the wall once more and lunged into it. She poured all of her strength into one long and controlled exhale, remembered from long ago days of Gyony training, and slowly the bricks began to give way. At first, the section of wall moved as a unit, one solid piece sliding away from the rest, but the moment the bricks were about halfway through they gave way into a cascade of mortar and stone. Portia collapsed into the pile of falling bricks and instinctively covered her head.

When the dust settled, she was surprised to find herself entirely unscathed. She shook the debris from her hair and clothes and took stock of her situation. The pile of rubble had spilled into another passageway that was entirely different from the one behind her. The new passage was a shorter hall with a domed ceiling that ended in a very sensible-looking oak door. She chanced one last glance into the endless corridor and saw that the knot of hair she'd left behind had finally fallen and was mostly buried in the detritus of broken bricks and chunks of lichen. She reached through the gaping hole in the wall and plucked it free, not willing to leave little bits of herself behind in the strange darkness.

The door opened easily, and she stepped through into a

plain little room. There was a single round window at the far side, through which shined a light so blindingly bright that she could not see out past it.

"Is this where you are? Have I found you?"

The silence was strained. Finally a quiet rustle came from behind the shaft of light.

"You have found me," said a voice that rustled and rasped like old paper. "Such as I am, and with what few tricks are left to me."

"Who are you?"

"Funny that you should ask, of all people."

Portia moved closer, gliding her feet as noiselessly as possible across the cold marble floor. "Why is that so funny?"

"Because you are the one who keeps me here. I was brought here for your purpose, yet you dare ask me who I am. You are cruel."

"I am not! And I did no such thing! Speak to me, tell me your name!"

"Name? I have none. Not anymore. No name save *Portia*. Portia Gyony, Nephilim of the Grigori. Portia, of the Penemue chapter house. Portia, beloved of Imogen. Portia defines me now, Portia describes me. None other, and nothing further. I am a pitiful echo of all that you are, now, *Portia*."

"I don't understand."

"Ah!" A shadow moved, arms flung outward in frustration. "Has my soul been thus wedded to a creature so daft? I was once something whole and entire, something made of all possibilities. And now I am just a shabby reflection, caught and confined in the soul of a simpleton."

She paused, her toenails glinting in the light that spilled in like the glow of a thousand moons. "I do not want to trouble you. I did not bring you here or bid you to stay. If I could let you go, you must know that I would."

"Let me go," the voice laughed dryly. "You could just as easily allow one of your limbs to go free if it grew tired of you. Or one of your eyes. Or the roots of your hair. Such fine hair it is. My memory is treacherous now, but I remember my last moments being separate from you. I remember your hair. Shining like a silver river flecked with starlight. I smelled your blood and knew you were kin to me. You were the offspring of my Brothers, a child of the Daughters of Men and the Sons of God. And I was afraid, because I realized then what was to become of me, what was to become of *us.*"

"You are a Nephilim too, then?"

"No, child, I am not."

"A *Bene 'elim*, then?"

"No. The *Bene 'elim* are naught but a higher order of Nephilim. They are what your Primacy consists of, what your Imogen is."

"Pardon me?"

"Imogen. She is so like you, yet so unlike. She is of purer stock than most, gifted with a higher degree of celestial blood. She is different from the Nephilim, she is *Bene 'elim*. You were born a *Bene 'elim* as well, a true Nephilim child of the union between a Son of God and a Daughter of Man. While her bloodline is older and more rarified, you are no less her equal. There are so few left. So few that both heaven and earth mourn it. Yet your Grigori takes steps most unnatural to change the courses of fate. Each creature that draws breath upon the earth must live and then die. Even *Bene 'elim* will die, though it might take hundreds, maybe thousands, of human years or more. The Nephilim flower far from the trunk, branching outward and ever outward, reaching steadily toward the transience of humanity. Soon, they will be no different from ordinary mortals."

"And you? You said you were neither Nephilim nor *Bene 'elim*. What does that leave?"

"*Banu ili*. I am a Child of God. Not fallen, not dead into mortality like the Nephilim."

"You are an angel, then?"

"I was."

"What are you now?"

The figure rose, silhouetted by the light. As it came toward her, she could see that it was a mirror of her height and body type. Portia stepped into the slanting golden beam to meet it and saw her own eyes, sharp and green, framed by silver lashes and crowned with silver brows. The young woman before her reached out her hands, her own familiar hands, and said in her own familiar voice, "I am you."

Spangled darkness became Portia's world for a moment, but as it cleared she saw that she stood facing the small oaken door at the far side of the room, with the light bathing her from behind. There was no one else with her. And she also saw that she cast no shadow.

"What do I do now?"

There was no answer, no echo. Only a surety of knowledge that she must climb out of this place on her own. She reached up for the window and found that it was open. The shaft of golden light seemed almost tangible enough to climb, at least as solid as to give her a boost, anyway. The window was a snug fit. She twisted and wriggled her shoulders through, and then her hips. The strange golden light enveloped her as she hoisted herself out of the darkness behind her and into whatever lay beyond it.

Pale blue light—not golden—surrounded her body, and tight silk bindings once again covered her eyes and mouth. But this was different.

Standing upright, she felt the aches and maddening itch of the monitors and diodes hooked into her flesh. She forced her breath to come smoothly through her nose, in deeply and out slowly, one after the other. The silk around her mouth was slick with saliva and her dry lips stuck to it. The division forced between her mind and her body was gone. She reached up, her arms moving easily at her command, and pulled the bandage away from her eyes. Wires snagged and snapped as she did so, and she brushed them away irritably.

Around her, the room slowly came into focus. The light shining into her own glass case made it difficult to see, but she could make out several of the cases around her, each containing one inanimate *Bene 'elim* adolescent. What was more, she could see the auras around each of them. Some were flickering and pale with the look of a creature barely holding onto life, while others were stronger. None of them felt right to her, however. None of these poor children would live very long, and the time they had would be filled with a numb cloud that divorced them from the unrelenting pain of their tortured, mangled bodies. She had to make it stop; the voice within her demanded it.

She pressed her hands against the glass of her enclosure, knocking and bumping here and there until she found the sliver-thin edge of the door. It fit so seamlessly into the wall that at first she could not see the perimeter. She had no idea how it closed or upon what kind of hinges it opened, but she did not care. She pressed her shoulder to it, just as she had to the craggy bricks of her dream. This wall gave way far more easily and Portia tumbled painfully to the floor in a tangle of tubes and wires and the narrow shift she wore. She tore loose the bindings wrapped around her head and methodically plucked each tiny diode from her skin. It reminded her of the time when, as a child, she'd spent hours picking at the scabs left over from her bout with the varicella pox.

Portia touched her chest, and below the flesh there she could feel the sigil burning like a brand. But she was shocked to find that her skin was whole and without a single trace of scarring. She thought of Imogen, who wore a symbol on her breastbone as well. But before she could set out to find her, Portia knew there was something she must do.

She followed the thickly corded electric wires that twined across the floor, leading from each of the specimen cases and converging to a single point at the far side of the room. The cloth-covered wires from the first dormitory also merged into the bundles as they ran down the walls. They all lead to a generator and a master control along the side wall. A tall copper-wrapped column emerged from the top of the turbine casing; it whined and sparked, casting violet-white shadows across the walls.

The wires came into the metal housing via a clear fused-quartz access port. The turbine cylinder behind the arcing column was similarly encased in the glassy fused quartz. The spinning magnets hummed inside the copper coiling, the electric current safely locked away behind the insulating crystal. The turbine shaft was connected through an opening in the bricks of the wall to a steam engine driven by a coal oven in the next room.

The control panel attached to the generator was a confusing array of brass and steel dials, buttons, sliders and switches. Not one of them was labeled. On a nearby rolling tray, Portia spied a bone saw. She dropped to her knees and isolated the power cords that lead away to the two nearest specimen cases. She sliced through the thick, rubber-coated wiring. Sparks flew as metal scraped metal and she was thrown back by a singularly large jolt that left her ears ringing and her palms smarting. At the far end of the room, two cases flickered and went dark.

Then the screaming began.

The two young men in the cases began to howl and thrash as whatever pain that had been kept at bay crashed down upon them with the force of a tidal wave. The inhuman keening chilled Portia, but she followed the wailing to the nearer case. The adolescent within sported bent and stunted wings of off-white feathers that erupted from large, crusted sores between his shoulder blades. His body trembled violently and she could see his eyes rolling beneath the tight bandage. Frothing spit began to ooze down his chin, leaving his broad chest looking almost inno-cently snow-flecked. His inhumanly elongated fingers clenched and unclenched, then very calmly he placed his palms against the glass. His quaking slowed and he tilted his head to one side as if listening. The wrenching cries subsided, but the stillness shattered as he slammed his forehead into the glass with as much might as he could muster. Again and again he repeated the gesture, until the sound of bone ringing off of glass was replaced by a hide-ous, wet noise that Portia was certain would haunt her dreams until the end of her days. Blood soaked the ban-dages completely and the poor lad's face was nothing more than a flattened ruin, but on and on he threw his head into the glass. Cracks formed, but the case did not shatter. Finally, after what seemed like hours, he slowly sank to his knees. His scalp had lifted from the bloodied pulp of his face and painted a swath of red on the glass in his wake.

The second young man stood as still as ever. But when Portia squinted her eyes, she could see his fingers and toes were black and miniscule wisps of smoke curled up from his nails. Electrocution. Portia prayed fervently that he had not suffered as much as his fellow.

But that left all the others. She could not bring herself to let each one die by some similarly gruesome method. She hunted the control panel for something she knew had to be there. A kill switch. It was not readily apparent, not some dangerous-looking red button nor some switch em-blazoned with a skull and crossbones. What she did find was an air-enrichment dial, one that regulated the flow of oxygen into each sealed chamber. Biting her lip, she turned the knob to zero.

"Saint Julitta, O Honored Matron, you once lost everything you had but held fast to your faith. You looked bravely upon the flames of your death, but God allowed your breath to leave you before you could suffer the pain of burning. Take the breaths of these children, these beloved *Bene 'elim,* and give them the peaceful death you were granted. Take their breath and with it, their pain. Escort them to the very gates of Heaven where they may claim their birthright and sing praises to the Most High. Amen. Amen. Amen."

One by one, the lights in the specimen cases dimmed and went out. There was no thrashing, no fighting for life. The sedatives in their timed little pumps kept each of the occupants calm and still as they slowly breathed their last and expired.

A single sob wracked her, but she forced herself to take a deep breath and wipe away her tears. Her heart broke not only for these nameless children, but for Imogen, who not only knew them, but loved them. She would be pleased to know that they suffered no longer. Or at least Portia hoped that she would.

She left the dark, dead specimen cases behind her.

The curtains no longer looked eerie and forbidding, lit as they had been with unearthly bluish light. They just hung listless and dusty, like shrouds. Portia passed through them and moved into the dormitory full of comatose children. There did not seem to be a master control in this room. She stood among them, listening to their hushed little breaths, barely audible beneath the click and whirr of the machines that kept them asleep.

She touched one girl's exposed forearm, and immediately her vision was flooded with springtime daylight; she could feel the damp crush of clover between her toes and taste the sweetness of air flushed with nectar. When Portia removed her hand, she was faced with the dim, stale dormitory and the dozens of filled beds. She crouched down and gazed into the girl's pale face. Her shadowed eyelids, webbed with red and blue veins, twitched and fluttered as she dreamed. Besides the mechanically induced rise and fall of her chest, it was her only body movement at all.

"At least you can dream, little one. I don't know what else I can do for you, but I wish there was something."

"Portia?"

Her head whipped around to the sound of the voice, so quickly the room spun. "Imogen!"

"How in the world did you get free?"

Portia shrugged, "It has something to do with what they did to me. Imogen, we have to get out of here, we need to get back home."

Imogen licked her lips nervously and nodded. "Not right now. They do not know you're not locked up! We must hide. Come with me, I know a good place." She reached out her hand and Portia took it. For a split second, she saw nothing but dazzling light. The brightness cleared and the world was made up of her and Imogen, a collage of images of their hands clasped, their lips pressed eagerly to one another, their hair mingling across the pillow, silver and gold.

The breath left her in a rush and she grabbed Imogen and held her tightly. Her body was whole and real once more, every inch familiar and warm.

"Come, my love, we mustn't dally here." She hooked her arm through Portia's and led her through the dormitory. They slipped through the tiny hall that ran between the kitchen and the dining room and came upon a small, hidden stair beside a water closet. The narrow switchback steps creaked under their weight, and Portia remembered crisp autumn mornings at Penemue when she and Imogen would climb into the apple larders and steal their breakfast from the fruit.

"Do you know where they took my Gladstone?"

"It's been emptied. The contents are in Lady Analise's study. I think the bag is there, too."

"Did they manage to get all that disgusting incubus blood off of it?"

Imogen glanced back over her shoulder, her mouth a thin line. "I don't know. Now hush, or we'll be caught!"

They climbed in silence, their footsteps quiet as a whisper on each step. Finally, they emerged in a round cupola overlooking an overgrown field behind the building. Far below them, tombstones seemed to grow among the tall grasses and climbing ivy. They were simple markers made of wood or stone, most in the form of unadorned crosses. These were the graves of the Sisters, Portia realized. The *Bene 'elim* children aged so slowly and never took sick—there would be no need for a burial ground for them. But the frail Sisterhood was all too human. She whispered a prayer under her breath for them, thanking them for their good stewardship of the children in their care, especially Imogen. Even though tragedy had befallen those darling charges, they had lived and now dreamed, securely loved. Portia envied them that security just a little. She turned back to Imogen who stood smiling, arms open to embrace her.

A small divan and a little side table sat beneath ribbons hung with dried herbs and flowers. Crystal prisms and iron keys also dangled from the cobweb-free rafters, spattering the room with glints of colored light. Imogen pulled her toward the divan and sat beside her. "This was my favorite hiding place," she whispered.

"I can see why. How long do you think we should stay up here?"

Imogen shrugged. The light outside was shifting toward late afternoon and drawing long shadows across the landscape. "Until morning at least. We can go just before first light, they won't expect that."

Portia nodded. "I agree." She smiled coyly. "Whatever shall we do until then?"

Imogen fluttered her eyelashes and looked a little shy. "I don't suppose anyone would find us up here, do you?"

"If they do, this is the way I want to die." Portia kissed her lips.

"Good," Imogen murmured and ran her fingers through Portia's shimmering hair.

Imogen's mouth was sweet and familiar. They fell against each other onto the divan. She reveled in the intimate softness of Imogen's yielding breasts, pushed up by her corset, and lost herself in the memory of how perfectly her mouth fit against the hollow at the base of Imogen's throat. The sensations were nearly overwhelming as Portia began to lose sense of herself.

This is the way I want to die, her echo from the dream

corridor came whispering to her. *I want to die. I want to die.*

"Darling, what's wrong?"

I want to die, the echo insisted, *I want to die.*

Portia shook her head to clear it. Imogen swam in her vision, growing blurry around the edges. For a moment, only a heartbeat's worth of time, she looked like Lady Hester. Portia blinked. "Imogen?"

"Yes, my love?"

I want to die...

Portia shakily got to her feet. "No."

Imogen reached out her hand and it seemed so familiar; the same shell-pink fingernails, the same dapple of honey-colored freckles across her knuckles, even the same crescent-shaped scar below her thumbnail from her first solo trial as a Gyony. It had been a *yōkai,* if Portia remembered correctly, and she had feared Imogen would lose the thumb. But there was something out of place. She gazed into Imogen's eyes, finding them achingly familiar yet somehow awry.

"Portia, beloved?"

"Saint Lucy," Portia prayed silently, "grant me true sight. Bring me your light, allow me your vision." When she opened her eyes, the aura around Imogen was dark, purple-black as a bruise. A demon's aura. "How dare you take *her* face and *her* voice?"

"Sweetheart...."

Portia backed away, coming up against the far wall of the little room altogether too quickly. "No, enough of your tricks. I won't be taken in by you again."

Imogen's forest-green eyes welled up with tears.

"Portia, please—"

Portia clenched her eyes shut. "No, no, damn it!"

"Oh, Portia, I don't know what they've done to you, but it must be so difficult."

Imogen glided from the divan and ran her fingers down Portia's cheek and along her jaw. She clasped both of Portia's hands in her own and brought them to her lips. Her breath hitched elegantly and she sighed across Portia's trembling fingers. Imogen smiled indulgently. "Portia, my love, you are safe here with me. No one knows where we are. Nothing is going to hurt you any-more, I won't allow it. " She opened her arms, beckoning. "Now, come here, my heart."

Portia allowed herself to be pulled back to the divan while scanning the room for a weapon. There was little at hand. Imogen settled into the plush seat, curling one lean leg beneath her and arranging her sage linen skirt in a pretty drape. She opened her arms, and Portia took her moment of opportunity. Knowing she would have but one chance, she grabbed Imogen's wrists and threw her to the floor. The young woman's body hit the floorboards with a *thud* of surprising density. Before she could recover, Portia pinioned her arms to the floor with her knees pressed into Imogen's biceps and her toes digging into Imogen's palms.

"Portia! What are you doing?"

"Calling you on your lie, you vile, demon-spawned *bitch*."

"Portia!" She struggled weakly, making heart-wrenching little mewling sobs.

"Stop it! Stop it now!" Portia grabbed the collar of Imo-

gen's shirtwaist and knocked her head back against the
floor.

"Please don't hurt me! Why are you hurting me,
Portia, my love? Portia, my only love?"

"Shut your mouth!" Portia hooked her fingers around the
mother-of-pearl buttons and wrenched the blouse open. She
scanned Imogen's chest, but found the sight only passing familiar; the corset was missing the monogram and the che-
mise was missing its lace. But that was not all that was out
of place. The sigil Portia had seen carved into Imogen's
flesh was not there. "Liar," Portia growled. "Liar!"

She wrapped her fingers around the slender neck she
once had kissed. But this was not Imogen's throat, she reminded herself.

Liar, the echo assured her.

Imogen laughed, first in her own warm, throaty voice,
but it soon warped into a harsh bray that rattled the glass in
the windows. "You think you are so clever, don't you? But I
have fooled you twice, now, and I have gotten a bit of a taste
for your blood, my dear." She bucked beneath Portia and
managed to knock her aside, then rose to her full height, a
frighteningly tall two yards and then some. Her knees bent
the wrong way and ended in splayed-toed feet with heavily
calloused skin. Glossy black talons scuffled at the floor as she
shifted her weight, and a thick web of flesh spanned the interiors of both her knee joints and her elbows. Her body was
sinuous and strangely genderless with a row of purple-
glossed, overlapping scales that ran from her chin to her pu-
bis. Her shock of violet-black hair grew from the top of her
head all the way down her back and along the top ridge of
her anxiously swishing tail. Portia knew that hidden in that

inky mass of hair was a pair of leathery wings tipped with poisoned spurs. She got to her feet, ready to dodge.

"Yes, you are a tasty little sugarplum." The succubus licked her lips with that terrifying, sinuous tongue; it roiled and twined in a prehensile fashion. She watched Portia with her slitted, predatory eyes. "There isn't anywhere for you to run. I made sure of that when I chose it." She smiled, and it was a grim expression that did nothing more than bend the edges of her wide mouth up at the corners. "Let's not make a fuss. Remember how easy and painless I made it for you before? You remember."

A wave of sleepy warmth wafted away from the succubus. Portia ignored it. "Actually, I don't."

The succubus lashed out with her razor sharp claws, but Portia brought her elbow up to block the attack. The demon's claws opened a slice on Portia's forearm that bled for a few seconds, then strangely healed on its own.

"I see the ritual was a success. I can smell that angel's soul locked up inside of you. Hmm, that is going to make you a little more difficult to subdue."

The succubus moved with surprising alacrity, her hands lashing out so quickly that Portia could not dodge her. Portia rolled as she hit the floor, coming up into a crouch. But the succubus was fast, launching herself at Portia's throat. Portia fell back and thrust her legs out, catching the demoness and knocking her off balance. As they both recovered, the succubus was first on her feet. The succubus clasped both hands together and landed an upward arcing blow to Portia's solar plexus that knocked her back into the wall. She sat, stunned and breathless, then staggered back to her feet.

"Strength," she breathed, thinking of the brick wall of her vision.

Strength!

She attacked the demoness, bringing her elbow sharply into the succubus' throat. The succubus gagged and coughed up a mouthful of steaming ichor that she spat into Portia's face. It was badly aimed and Portia ducked it easily, coming up for another hit. But the succubus was ready for this one and deflected Portia's attack to the left, sending her sprawling into the window.

The glass shattered around her, falling around her face and shoulders like terrible rain. Her blood flowed and spattered the glittering shards with red before the myriad wounds closed up and healed themselves. She remained bent over, panting into her bosom. In her right hand she gripped a large, jagged shard of glass.

The succubus came toward her, baited. Portia forced herself to breathe deeply, to calmly wait for just the right moment.

"Poor sugarplum," the succubus rasped. "I thought you'd be more trouble, actually. I suppose the Gyony reputation is a lie, just like the rest of the Grigori's teachings. I have trapped you for a second time now, and not even broken a sweat." She clucked her tongue and laughed.

Portia whirled around and slashed the shard across the succubus' side, opening the flesh a half an inch deep. Blood flowed at once, puce and brackish, sticky with ichor. The creature howled and made to pounce but Portia was too quick. Ignoring the sharp glass edges that bit deeply into her own flesh, Portia ducked low into a shoulder roll and came up with the blade once more, driving it between two of the succubus' belly scales. The shard snapped off in the wound, and the demoness shrieked until the rest of the windows broke. Portia fought the swoon that threatened to pull her into unconsciousness. It was a succubus' last resort, that keening wail that could incapacitate an assailant, giving the demoness a chance to run, or to kill.

"I am stronger than you think, Lamia."

The succubus looked genuinely surprised. "You know my name?"

Portia saw the glimmer of her advantage and took it. "Lamia, I cast thee back into the depths of hell from whence you came! Be banished, demon, I know your name! By the will of the Archangel Michael, I banish thee! I banish thee, Lamia!" Portia stretched out her right hand, glistening with her own fresh blood, and it glowed with a burst of white-hot light. In a few quick strides she covered the small space and touched her palm to Lamia's breastbone. "In Michael's name, be gone, demon! In my name, Portia Gyony, be gone demon! Lamia, be banished!"

The light all but exploded from her hand, widening into a glaring ball like a star in the center of the room. It enveloped the succubus like a shell. The demon's screams were muffled and grew fainter until they were nothing but a tinny twang, like the song of the cicada. "Be gone, demon, and with you all of your foul tricks and false faces. Never make a mockery of the ones I love again. So do I will it to be." The carapace of light began to crack, opening with great fissures and chasms along the surface. The echo within her began to hum with pleasure and power. *"So do I will it to be. Be gone, demon."*

The crystalline sheath of light encasing the succubus shattered into brilliant fragments that hovered a moment in the air before swirling to the floor in the cold evening breeze. Portia stood in the center of the room, alone save for the soft moan of the wind through the broken windows and the thrumming of might in her soul.

She spat into the dust that had once been a succubus and went in search of the real Imogen.

7

A low beat vibrated through Portia's breast-bone. It was not the echo, the splintered soul that had been bound to her. It came from without. As she navigated the twists and turns of the old nunnery she could feel it fade, and then sharpen in intensity. It throbbed in concert with something else, a sympathetic vibration somewhere else in the vast building, and the closer she got, the more intense the feeling and the more desperate she became to unite with this sister sensation. A subtle radiance emanated from her breastbone and she knew that this was how she would find Imogen, who wore a matching sigil wedding her flesh to her soul.

She came upon a long hall two floors below the cupola tower and paused to rest a moment before continuing on. Dark cherry wood paneled the hall, and a long strip of carpet ran down the center. Although the rug looked little used, it was ragged along the edges where rats and mice had gnawed off yarn to build their nests. But the carpet, as well as the rest of the corridor, was free of dust and cobwebs. It was the first clean area she'd encountered since coming down from the tower room. She immediately went on guard and felt dreadfully exposed in her short linen shift. At least this one fit better than the last one had.

Treading carefully, she inched her way through the

hall, coming to a door at the far end. Light showed all around it, the kind of striking brilliance that could only come from electricity. She crouched before the keyhole and peered inside. What she saw looked like a library. The rich paneling continued within, and there were shelves along the wall opposite her and a large table with thickly carved legs in the center of the room. It also appeared to be empty, even though all the lights were on. It looked so much like the library at Penemue, Lady Hester's library. The pang of memory surprised Portia, it was so sudden and so fierce. She hastily dashed away her tears and refocused her energy. She could not sense anyone inside, but the insistent beat pleaded to her and commanded her, assuring her that what she sought lay in this room.

The door opened without a sound, and Portia crouched beside the doorframe ready to bolt or to fight, but after a few excruciatingly tense moments of silence, she dared to peek in. The room was empty. Bookcases and glossy dark tables furnished the handsome library. The subtle hint of cigar smoke permeated the leather of the wingback chairs and the ochre plaster of the walls. Portia slid into the room, closing the door behind her with only the smallest *click* of the latch. Books and scrolls lay open across the trestle table, along with a large journal beside an inkwell and pen stand. The journal was open and Portia could see notes, diagrams, and a long list of familiar symbols and sigils. With her fingernails, she lifted a few of the preceding pages and found them similarly filled. The writing was elegant and bold, the letters marching in perfect rows across each creamy page. She knew this handwriting; she knew it very well. How many times had he left notes filled with scathing taunts pushed under her door? And he always signed them, the arrogant bastard.

Leaving the journal on the table, she turned to scan the rest of the room. At the far side, between windows that also overlooked the little graveyard, what she saw shocked her. Her duster hung like a museum artifact from a wooden rod attached to the wall. Its sleeves stretched out on either side as if beckoning to her for its release. Beside it was mounted her crossbow, and a half dozen Blessed-wood stakes were arrayed beneath it. Below it all was a pedestal on which sat her Gladstone bag, completely clean of the incubus' blood, although care had obviously been taken to preserve the patina and staining of the leather. It stood open with its contents artfully arranged on little risers. Front and center on the pedestal was a braid of her hair coiled neatly on a black velvet pillow. A card at the right corner read: *Portia Gyony, personal effects.*

She took a step back and realized that she was shaking. The pulsing beat in her chest remained steady and relentless, and when she turned to follow its heavy tug, she collapsed slowly to her knees. The glass case in front of her was similar to those that had held the experimented-upon Pure Children downstairs, but this one was far more decorative. It was fitted with chased bronze moldings depicting winged women drawn with graceful curves and sinuous hair surrounded by stylized flowers and leaves.

Imogen stood behind the wall of crystal wearing nothing but a diaphanous golden gown that billowed into soft drapes at the low neckline and at her feet. Her hair had been drawn back from her face and spilled softly down her shoulders with a few curls left to dance against her cheeks. Her eyes were open and as glassy as any doll's. She stared straight ahead of her, focused on a door across the room. Two cards marked her case. The first read simply: *The body of Imogen Gyony, lineage of the BENE 'ELIM (Pure Children)*. The second was placed below it: *Successful experiment in body/soul manipulation. Imogen Gyony (BENE 'ELIM/Pure Children) in suspended animation, body and soul housed in one vessel, timeless and enduring*. Next to the text was a line drawing of the sigil that was easily visible on Imogen's chest.

She gazed at the first label a long moment before the meaning of what it said fully dawned. *The body of Imogen Gyony*. When Imogen was killed, Nigel had stolen her body and brought it here as some sort of trophy. All the years that Imogen's ghost had been Portia's companion, her body had been standing here like a mannequin in her childhood home. Portia thought she was going to vomit. She sank to her knees and waited for the debilitating wave of nausea to pass.

What do I do now? Should she try to rescue Imogen, or should she make her escape to the chapter house and bring back help? Imogen did not seem to be in any danger, but Portia was loath to leave her beloved in such circumstances. Katriel's voice haunted her within a slip of memory: *"Master Nigel is keeping care of her."*

Livid, Portia rose to her feet, wanting nothing more than to tear Nigel limb from pompous limb. Behind the door across from the glass case, she was not surprised in the least to find his bedroom, or to see that Imogen's carefully crafted smile and gentle gaze fell directly onto his bed.

She could almost see Nigel languidly fondling himself in bed while Imogen beamed down on him, trapped not only within those wretched glass walls but also within the confines of her own body, unable to close her eyes or look away. Keeping care indeed.

Portia gripped the doorknob with white-knuckled anger, her heartbeat roaring in her ears in time with the now-familiar throb just above it.

"Whatever are you doing in my room?" Nigel's voice sliced through her, shearing her to the core. She could hear that he was genuinely surprised, and when she turned her head, she saw why.

Nigel stood beside another door, one that had been mostly obscured by a globe and a tall potted palm. He wore a banyan robe and a thick towel wrapped around his waist. His ebony hair dripped from the bath and hung in stringy spirals nearly to his shoulders. But what took Portia's breath away was not his pale and nearly naked body, but what was on it. Intricate patterns of scars intertwined with inked tattoos across his chest and down his torso, disappearing beneath the towel. They were a mass of arcane symbols and Enochian script blended together and carved into his flesh.

For a long moment neither of them moved; mutual shock and confusion held them fast. Portia appraised her situation. She was alone in a strange room with no form of weapon near at hand. Although Nigel was not armed or dressed, she had a bad feeling about what those tattoos and scars meant and did not want to try to best him with magic.

Her window of opportunity began to close as Nigel

took a step toward her. He closed off the space between the table and the wall with his body, moving with feline grace and intimidation. Portia straightened her spine but stepped back from him, her mind reeling with options. Echoes bounced chaotically through her. From somewhere distant she could hear Imogen crying, but in the glass case Imogen just smiled demurely as if nothing in the world was amiss.

Nigel continued to advance on Portia, a slow smile spreading across his face. "Well, hello little foster-sister, how good it is to see you." With one hand he closed the robe over his exposed body, and with the other he began to unwind the towel and unencumber his legs.

"You are looking well, Nigel," Portia stalled, hoping to retreat far enough to reach her crossbow or anything from her bag.

"That's good. Because I have never felt better." His grin turned predatory as she smiled, wracking her brain for some other dull pleasantry to distract him. "Never in my life."

He covered the dozen feet between them faster than Portia was able to see. With his full weight and speed behind him, he slammed her into a wingback chair at the end of the long table. The chair rocked backward and fell over, sending Nigel sprawling on top of her. They landed in a tangle in the curve of the overturned chair.

His bare flesh against hers terrified her as he locked his legs around her torso. "I have been wondering, my sweet, when I would get my chance with you. The Lady Analise sees things one way, but I have another vision. You and I are unique, Portia. What we could produce together would rival the forces of heaven and earth."

"What are you talking about?"

Nigel tilted his head down and parted his hair. Along the scalp there was a line of silver beneath where the dye had grown out. "It took some cunning and spellwork to create a permanent dye, but I managed. I am terribly clever, you know. And you do realize what this means, don't you, sweet sister? I am a half-breed, too. Just like you. In fact, I could very well be your brother. How many *Banu ili* do you suppose are around these parts? Besides poor stupid Katriel, the castrated old fool." Nigel laughed to himself as if he had happened upon some memory that amused him. "Angels have no ability to control the world of the dead. Did you know that? The Aldias are the only celestial beings that have that influence, and it was hard-earned, I assure you. This power was what Katriel wanted desperately. So we promised him his every wish and he willingly sold his soul to the Aldias." Nigel grinned broadly, showing his teeth. "And we made him our slave. Handy to have around, too. A personal angel at your beck and call. But our father, he was different. He was a crafty, powerful sort."

"Nigel, you cannot know we have the same father."

His dark brows furrowed. "This is my story. I shall tell it how I please. Besides, who has been the one doing the re-search, hmmm?" He indicated the table full of books and pa-pers. "And what I have concluded is that a child of our getting would be, with a little assistance, twice as power-ful as you or me." He ground his hips against her stomach. "And oh, the possibilities." He glanced up at Imogen, who gazed back with an approving smile. But Portia thought she saw tears in her beloved's eyes.

"Nigel…"

"You're just afraid, sweet sister. You have never been with a man. I know the incubus tried his hardest, but I guess it just was not hard enough!" He barked with laughter at his own joke and thrust against her. His arms were braced on the chair's sides and his elbows were locked; Portia saw her chance.

She shrank away from him, sliding back toward the seat of the chair and bracing her feet beneath her bent legs. The linen shift rode up, exposing her nudity to him from toes to armpits. He leaned forward, his gaze hungry. Portia whimpered softly in submission and saw Nigel's pupils dilate with lust, leaving only a thin ring of grey around them.

He forgets what the name Gyony means, she mused.

What the name Gyony means, replied the echo.

She struck out with her arms, slamming them into the tender crook of his elbows. His arms gave way and he dropped toward her, but not before she tucked her chin to her chest and met his face with the top of her skull. His nose crumpled against her head and blood began to flow like a crimson river into her hair, dripping down into her eyes. Nigel bellowed with pain. Portia sprang from the seat cushion, but Nigel grabbed her around the hips. She twisted and fought, writhing and kicking, aiming for the swelling center of his face. If he was half as powerful as he claimed, the injury would soon heal itself, but she hoped it would buy her enough time to flee. Her knee connected with his chin. She wedged her legs against his chest and kicked him aside, all under Imogen's artificial smile.

Once free of him, she scrambled to her feet, tugging the shift down over her body, hating that he had seen her so exposed. As she ran for the door, she flung an arm across the table. Scrolls and pages flew everywhere and she heard the grating sound of the cut-glass inkwell breaking open against the floor.

"No! You cursed, wretched daughter of a—"

She did not catch the rest. Portia threw herself out the door and slammed it shut behind her. She dashed headlong down the long corridor and toward the stairs. There were more rooms below, rooms in which she thought she could hide. Except she could feel him behind her, scenting her trail as easily as a hound would. He would find her no matter where she hid; he would take his time and he would hunt her down. She needed to find somewhere to make a stand. Somewhere with good cover, a weapon, and clothes.

Through another corridor and down a flight of steps tucked into the corner of the building, Portia came across a familiar room. White walls with tall windows surrounded a half-dozen wrought-iron cots, also painted white. She had been brought here after Lamia's first seduction. A chest of drawers and an armoire stood on the far side of the room. Portia went at once to find something to put on that would offer more protection than the flimsy shift. She found a pair of cotton pantalets trimmed in rotten lace and an old-fashioned corset spotted with rust, the kind with heavy steel boning laid edge to edge. It was the next best thing to armor. She put it on over the shift and pantalets, lacing it tight and secure. At the back corner of the armoire she found a few pairs of shoes and boots, many mismatched. Stockings were not in evidence, so she crammed her bare feet into a pair of battered brown boots that looked near enough to her size.

Behind her, a glass-fronted medicine cabinet stood near the beds. Inside were jars of camphor and smelling salts, several filled syringes, and about a half-dozen scalpels. They were the same kind Analise had used, a small but deadly sharp crescent-shaped blade affixed to the end of a slender metal handle about a hand's breadth in length. Portia coiled her hair into a quick bun and slipped four scalpels through it, using their handles like hair pins and letting the sharp blades jut out. She took the fifth in her hand, along with two syringes tipped with thick copper needles. She had no idea what liquid was inside them, save that it was clear, slightly viscous, and there was an awfully good chance it contained a sedative. On the bottom shelf of the cabinet was a black leather doctor's bag. It looked a bit like a miniature version of her Gladstone. She tossed in the camphor, the smelling salts, all the gauze she could find, and a silver matchbox she found sitting on one of the window sills. She slipped her arm through the bag's handle and, keeping a scalpel at the ready, made her way back out toward the main corridor.

She had barely left the room when she was forced to slip back inside. Someone was heading her way. Ducking behind the open door, she slowly and gently set the bag on the floor and retrieved a syringe. She held the scalpel in her right hand—tilting it so the blade flashed nicely in the light—and the syringe in her left, held low and out of immediate view.

Katriel came in, humming. Portia pounced as soon as he fully entered the room. She kicked the door closed behind them and brought her arm around his shoulders, pressing the point of the scalpel to his throat.

"Do not make a sound," she growled, nicking open a small wound atop his voicebox.

Ever so gently, Katriel gave a slight nod.

"Tell me where I may find Lady Analise. I would like to pay a call on her. She and I have some unfinished business to discuss and it is most pressing, you understand."

The fallen angel nodded once more. "Downstairs," he whispered. "In the Mother Superior's office. She is there now. I only left her moments ago."

"Excellent." Portia stabbed the syringe into the side of his neck.

Katriel stiffened. "Wait, I can help you. Trust me and take me with you, and I will do whatever you ask. I was tricked into coming here and I am now trapped. I was a fool and I have paid for my recklessness. Please, Spirit-Sister, have mercy on me."

"No." Portia depressed the copper plunger, and after only a few seconds Katriel slumped against her, then collapsed to the floor.

She snatched up the doctor's bag and made straight for the Mother Superior's chambers.

8

Lady Analise Aldias had surrounded herself with lamps of electric light tethered with black snaking wires that ran along the ceiling and walls of the vaulted chamber like vines. Portia crouched just to one side of the spill of harsh white light that cut across the dim and tranquil hallway. Within, Lady Analise seemed to be making a wax cylinder dictation recording. She spoke plain, slow words into a recording device.

"No," she enunciated, "I do not believe that Hester Edulica ever caught on that her communications to and from the Primacy were being disrupted and replaced by our own correspondence, do you? If you do, then you're a greater fool than I ever thought. The Primacy has never made any claim of suspicion that their contact with the Penemue chapter house was anything but legitimate. I believe we have been successful in significantly weakening Penemue's ties with the Primacy, and now would be an ideal time to take action and claim both the chapter house and the village."

To Portia's surprise, a voice answered Analise. "And my payment?" It sounded canned and grainy, a woman's voice that was unfamiliar to her.

"The Aldias keep their promises, my dear Mistress Miniver, do they not? I will send word to Lady Claire right away."

"And then I will be accepted into the Aldias? You will teach me your magic?"

"Did I not say as much before?" Butter would not have melted in Analise's mouth.

There was a long pause. "We are agreed, then. The Lady Hester's body was disposed of and I have secreted away some of her ashes for you."

"Ah, very resourceful, Miniver. Deliver that as well to Lady Claire, will you?" Analise made some notes in a leather-bound book similar to Nigel's. "What of the other? The man, Emile."

"Problematic. He may have to be dispatched as well."

Miniver, if Portia recalled correctly, was the village midwife. She was not personally familiar with the woman, but she remembered that Emile had summoned her along with Lady Claire Aldias to treat Lady Hester's illness. They had been working with Nigel and Analise all along. And Emile was now in danger from them. Portia nervously ran her thumb along the handle of the scalpel.

"Very well. Monitor him, but do nothing until I next contact you. Is that clear, Miniver?"

"Yes, m'lady."

"I shall be calling again at the same time next week. Do not make me wait, Miniver, is that understood?"

"Yes, m'lady!"

"Signing off," Analise said briskly and switched off the machine. She sat back in her prim desk chair. The sound of her pen scratching across the expensive paper went on for several long minutes as she hummed softly.

Portia felt warm breath on the back of her neck. The sudden pressure of hands on her shoulders, while gentle, was terrifying. "Found you," Nigel whispered, lips brushing against her ear. "What have we here, sweet sister?" He drew out one of the scalpels crammed through her bun. "You are up to something nefarious, aren't you?"

At the edge of her vision, Portia could see that Nigel's face was perfect and unscathed. The only hint of the struggle was a film of dried blood ringing the edges of both nostrils. He was dressed now, wearing a crisp white shirt buttoned to the throat and tan trousers with black suspenders. He looked disturbingly normal, and Portia was almost convinced she had imagined the twining scars and tattoos down his torso, except that she had felt them against her own belly as he pressed against her.

Nigel twirled the scalpel as easily as a pencil, heedless of its gleaming sharp edge. "Were you meaning to do something with these?" When he saw that she was not going to answer him, he put his hands on her shoulders once more. "Portia, I must confess, there is no love lost between the Lady Analise and myself. As I mentioned, she and I have disagreed on many things, the first of which is your treatment. I give you my word that I will lend you my aid in her destruction."

"Nigel, you'll forgive me if I do not believe you."

"I understand." His smile was deceptively disarming. "Here"—he patted her cheek—"let me show you. And afterward, you and I will be the ones to make the decisions." He rose and strolled into the room, his thumbs hooked into his front pockets.

"Nigel, what excellent timing! I was about to send for you." Analise shut her book and stood. "I have received news from Penemue. Everything has gone according to plan. Hester is dead and we have her ashes in our possession. The only thing that remains to be dealt with is that glorified nanny, Emile. But Miniver assures me that she and Claire have the situation well in hand. Within the month, Penemue will be ours, and then we can move on to our next step."

Nigel wandered the room, nodding and touching things seemingly at random.

"Are you listening to me, Nigel?"

"What? Oh, yes. But I'd rather you stop talking."

Analise sputtered. "Excuse me, young man?"

"You damned magpie, I said, *stop talking.*" He raised his hand to her and it flashed with light and shadow simultaneously. Analise doubled over, clutching at her throat. Nigel chuckled. "So, you see, *my Lady*, I thank you for your efforts and your successes, but I believe we are finished with one another."

The woman sank to the floor and clawed at her own throat, raking bloody welts with her fingernails.

"You see, little Analise, your vision is so narrow. And you don't know half of the potential of the Aldias. Or if you do, you make precious little use of it. Do you remember your assistant? What was his name...*Maynard*, that's right. Maynard. How could I forget? He was the one who showed me the books and how to use them, how to *really* use them." Nigel slowly slipped his suspenders from his shoulders, letting them hang down over his hips. He unbuttoned his shirt and shrugged free of it, allowing it to drape from his waistband. The markings on his body showed ghost-like through his undershirt. He rubbed his palms over his stomach and ribs. "And he unlocked the secret of the blood."

Analise struggled and her face flushed red.

"Not only the blood magic, the carving of the flesh, the use of symbols. He taught you that. And I have seen what you've done with it, with Portia. But there was another way. The other road to power Maynard did not share with you, not like he did with me. Maynard shared everything with me: his knowledge, his secrets, his body, his blood, and finally, his soul. He gave it all to me." Nigel glanced up at Portia, who crouched in the doorway, aghast. "And when this is finished, my sweet sister, I will share it all with you."

Analise gurgled and gagged, her flesh purpling slowly. Her lips began to grow as ashen as her slate-grey hair.

Nigel went to his knees and took Analise's chin in his hands, forcing her gaze to meet his. "And now, dear mistress, I will show you the extent of Maynard Aldias' teachings."

A low, droning ululation emanated from Nigel's throat, and with it a dark violet glow. He leaned forward and pressed his mouth against Analise's. And then he drew in a deep breath through her mouth. As he did, Analise's flesh began to pucker and sink into the hollows of her bones. Her cheeks collapsed first, followed by her supple throat, the skin cleaving to the straining tendons. Nigel drew out her very life in one profound inspiration after another. Portia could hear, over the hideous noises Nigel still made, a peculiar creak and snap, not unlike the sounds tree branches often made during a storm. It came from beneath Analise's skirt. It grew louder and more intense, and then Portia saw its cause as Analise's fingers began to wither. The flesh shrank into wizened grooves, growing tighter until the bones within snapped. Nigel breathed in every tiny bit of her essence, all the way to the tips of her fingers. And once the fingers were drained of life, they began to crumble. Her fingernails fell off first, drifting to the floor like autumn leaves, followed by the rest of her hands, bit by bit.

Nigel's chest expanded, stretching wider than any human's Portia had ever seen. He suckled loudly, as if trying to wrest every last drop from Analise's desiccated body. When he finally let her go, what had once been Lady Analise Aldias disintegrated into dry, dusty fragments dressed in a blue silk frock. Nigel remained hunched over, panting. Portia raced forward, snatching a second scalpel from her hair and wielding one in each hand. She lashed her right hand across Nigel's neck, opening a deep cut from his ear to his collarbone. With her left, she stabbed forward, burying the scalpel into his closed eye, feeling the tip grind against the back of the socket.

The second scalpel stuck fast, and she brought the first one abruptly upward, laying open his throat while she reached for another weapon. She pulled it from the bottom and it only came free with a tug and a shower of hair. Portia sought to jab one scalpel between his ribs and continue to slash at his face with the other. If she could keep wearing him down, there was no way he could heal all the wounds. She made contact with his side, but the scalpel shattered in her hand when the tip touched one of the sigils. She wrenched the last blade free of her hair and wished she had decided to try her luck with the remaining syringe.

Nigel knocked her aside with only the slightest touch. Portia fell hard onto her backside but had her feet beneath her again in an instant. She came at Nigel once more, feinting left, hoping to draw the attention of his right hand while she aimed for a spot of skin that was bare of tattoos. She did not get within arm's reach before whatever force he summoned knocked her down again. She tumbled back over her shoulder and lay winded for a split second before regaining her legs once more.

Nigel was on his feet. He had plucked the scalpel from his eye and was holding his neck. The unearthly sound still reverberated from him, and his chest was still most unnaturally enlarged. His breath came in short bursts and his skin glimmered with a sheen of sweat.

"The Gyony have trained you well." He spoke while he hummed. "And perhaps if you had not been so careless with Katriel, leaving him helpless and sedated right where I could find him, you *might* have had a chance against me, albeit a small one. I have always been able to take care of myself, you know. Even when I was a child, I was quite a powerful being. Katriel was a powerful being, even if the Aldias did own what remained of his pitiful, ragged soul. It was tasty nonetheless, that soul, like sucking the sweet marrow from a bone. Thank you for leaving him for me, Portia, so defenseless and tender, just waiting for my appetite. This is the secret Maynard taught me. It cost me much to learn, but what is a small thing like virginity weighed against the balance of this power? Besides, I got it back, after a fashion. He tasted of peat and cold autumn nights. And Analise..."—his eyes, both now functioning even if one was rimed with blood, rolled back in ecstasy—

"she was more delectable than I could have ever imagined. In my wildest dreams—and my dreams are indeed wild—I never imagined that her soul could taste so delicious. Like peaches rolled in cloves and honey. And my tongue trembles with anticipation to taste you, my sister, just a little taste. I can smell it on you, cherry blossoms and ginger"—his nostrils flared inhumanly wide—"and tart green apples." Saliva moistened the corners of his mouth.

His breathing was still rough, almost labored. His ribcage flexed, stretching and compressing like a bellows. The tattoos and scars became more evident through the over-stretched undershirt. She could see his pulse beating hard in his neck and temples and she could feel it dimly in a rhythmic shadow of the throb behind her own breastbone. He seemed to have grown even larger.

"Ah, sweet sister, I couldn't consume you. Not until you gave me enough children to complete my plan. I dare not yet dream what they will taste of, but I yearn for it already."

Portia slowly slid one step back, and then another. "Nigel," she began, not knowing what she could possibly say to him. "Nigel, is this what you want? A trail of death that ends at your feet?"

His voice was deeper now, darker, somehow incorporating the hum. His jaws had thickened, distorting the sound. "What I want at my feet is the *world*. We have lived banished to the shadows for too long, for millennia. Why should we defend humanity when they seek and have always sought to destroy us? Analise and the rest of them, they always thought too small. They wanted to undermine the Primacy and take control of the Grigori.

But that still leaves us trotting at the heels of humanity like dogs. But no longer! The Aldias tried to orchestrate the makeup of the Nephilim. They spliced genes, they implanted souls, they searched tirelessly for centuries to find this place in order to tap into this undiluted bloodline of what they termed the 'Pure Children,' the true Watchers, the *Bene 'elim.* Short-sighted." He snorted. "I prefer the long view. And you will, as well."

Portia continued to move toward the door. She did not like her chances against this new Nigel. The old Nigel had been bad enough. She knew her only hope lay in reaching her gear in his room. He needed nothing so much as a Blessedwood bolt in his head. She needed a distraction, something to give her enough time to make the dash back to his grotesque exhibition, and to Imogen.

"So, what do you have planned, then? How are you going to do this differently than *she* did?" Portia nodded toward the grisly pile of what once had been Lady Analise.

Nigel leaned back against Analise's writing table, considering. It creaked ominously beneath his growing bulk. His face was smooth and untroubled, both eyes gleaming grey above his broadening cheekbones. The only signs of trauma to his thickly muscled neck were raw red welts, nothing serious. Portia sidled up to him, schooling her features into a smiling, calm mask. She opened herself to the echo within, feeling the power of it surge easily into her fingertips. She did not think the encasement in which she'd trapped Lamia, the succubus, would hold Nigel, but it might buy her just enough time.

He spoke, but Portia could not hear him; she was listening to the rush of light in her ears. She pressed both of her palms into his chest. His heart beat erratically and his ribs strained. It was as if there was something inside of him attempting to come out. In the shadow of Nigel's heartbeat, Portia could hear an echoing voice. Something was there within him, as there was a celestial being within her, but his was thumping, dark, and violent. It was dangerous; it was demonic. It wanted nothing more than to do her harm.

Rape her. Consume her. Rape her. Consume her, it rasped. *Her strength, her power, her soul! Take them from her!*

Portia channeled all the fierce heat and light within her at Nigel. She was not a magus by nature or by training, and for a moment he resisted, clenching his teeth, but the dreadful light finally surrounded him. Portia could easily feel his strength barely contained within the enveloping glow and knew that she could not destroy him this way. She could hear his muffled cries as she ran upstairs, fleeing as if all the demons in hell were on her heels. For all she knew, in a few moments, they would be.

—9—

Portia went straight for her crossbow. It pained her to run past Imogen, but she'd be much more able to defend them both with a range weapon. She nocked a bolt and pulled the rest off the wall and threw them into the Gladstone. She quickly packed all the other articles that Nigel had punctiliously laid out in his unwholesome little shrine. Among the items was her Saint Christopher medallion. She could feel her spell still working in it. *Whoever shall behold the image of Saint Christopher shall not faint or fall on that day.* It was without its chain, so she slipped it into her corset, nestling it between her breasts.

An ominous rumble shook the floor, urging her on. She dumped the contents of the doctor's bag in as well and yanked her duster down. She shrugged into it and threw the Gladstone across her shoulder as if it were any other day. She felt better at once, familiar and in control. Only then did Portia turn her attention to Imogen. Moving quickly, she found no discernable door in the glass.

"Imogen, shut your eyes!" Portia did not wait to see if her lover complied. She pulled out the bolt and rammed the butt of her crossbow into the case over and over again. Spidery cracks spread out from the small, jagged hole she created, but the glass would not break.

Portia reached for the wingback chair, still toppled

onto the floor. She hefted it with ease, surprised by her own strength, but before she could heave it into Imogen's glass prison, a thunder-like peal moved through the building once more, rattling the books and curios on the shelves. It was followed by a piercing preternatural howl. Nigel, or what was left of him, had broken free. The chair fell to the ground, forgotten, as Portia clapped her hands over her ears to blot out the sound. The windows and cabinets around the room hummed and sang along with the roiling yowl emanating from the Mother Superior's office below.

At long last, the glass of Imogen's cell shattered, along with every other breakable item in the room. The deafening wail broke off sharply, but it took a moment for Portia to notice the silence beneath the ringing in her ears.

Glass littered the room, some pieces powder-fine, others large and jagged. Portia picked her way over to Imogen, who stood still and smiling with glittered shards frosting her cheeks, hair, and eyelashes like snowflakes. Gently, Portia ran her fingertip along the inside of Imogen's eyelids before closing them and brushing away the glass. Imogen remained doll-like and pliant.

Portia heard a loud but distant *thud,* and then another, each one growing louder, closer. Footsteps, she reasoned, and heavy ones at that. She pulled Imogen free of the broken cell and carried her into the bedroom. She laid her down and began to inspect her flesh for any kind of marking that would be keeping her in this state. The footsteps came nearer. Portia could hear the treads of the stairs creaking, often breaking, beneath the strain of whatever creature headed toward them.

With trembling hands, Portia pulled Imogen's tawdry dress aside and searched her familiar skin once more, but to no avail. Portia would hear her assailant panting at the far end of the corridor. Panicked, she rolled Imogen over, meaning to start her search a third time when she saw them: two small sigils carved into the soles of Imogen's feet. Delicately, Portia sliced an X through each one with her last remaining scalpel.

Imogen's muscles relaxed, and she sank into the bedding with a long sigh. For a moment, Portia feared she has destroyed the wrong signs, but the steady beat that mirrored her own heart's remained strong. Slowly, far too slowly as the splintering groan of heavy feet on wood drew ever nearer, Imogen pushed herself up off the bed and sat back on her knees.

"You must listen carefully, Portia, we will have but few chances at him."

"Him?"

"That sound you hear. I know what it is. And I know *why* it is." She turned to look at Portia, her eyes haunted with shadow. "The books on his table. Hurry, bring them here."

Portia hesitated a moment before bringing back the books, the scrolls, and the journal, each spattered with ink and covered in glass grit. Imogen took them at once and began to page through.

"He carved himself up in front of me. He wanted me to see." She smiled wryly. "But I don't think he expected me to be able to use it against him."

"Do you understand any of this?" Portia's skill with cryptography, sigils, and glyphs was limited to what she had been taught in her younger years at the knee of her Aldias teacher, mostly a smattering of charms and spells calling on various angels and saints.

Imogen nodded, her eyes still scanning the pages in quick succession. "We were taught magic. And lots of it." She paused and glanced up. "Portia, I was only a Gyony for you, because they wanted me to stay close to you. I am not sure how it was done. I was certain I failed the trials, but somehow I became a warrior. I tried my best at it. You must know, Portia, it was not your fault that I died. I was never meant to be a Gyony. I am a terrible fighter."

Portia was surprised to find tears on her cheeks. "What are you saying?"

Imogen laid the book aside to put her arms around her. "That there was nothing you could have done. When you stepped away from me to face the *langsuir*, you should have been able to trust me to cover you as you would trust any other Gyony. The demon sensed my weakness, and it came straight for me. It knew I was a fraud, and it took its advantage. It was not you who failed me. I failed you. And I am so sorry. My love, you always did right by me. Even now, after all of this. Let me return the favor." Her kiss melted away Portia's fear, filling her with a warm sense of calm. "Keep him distracted for as long as you are able. Go."

A weight suddenly lifted from Portia's being, an old wound breaking open to vent its purulent contents and finally heal properly. She held onto Imogen a moment longer, savoring the feel of her, solid and real, in her arms once more, relishing the evaporation of guilt and shame she had carried for far too long. "I love you," she whispered.

Taking up her weapons and readying a crossbow bolt, Portia walked resolutely to the bedroom door. She turned back. Imogen was watching her go. "Imogen, I want you to know, you have never dishonored the name of the Gyony." She shut the door and moved into the main room to establish a defensible position.

After moving several of pieces of furniture in front of the door and spreading a liberal sprinkling of the most jagged glass shards she could find across that half of the room, Portia climbed onto the sturdy table. She fortified her position with one of the wingback chairs and crouched behind it, taking careful and steady aim at the door. She waited. In the early years of her training, her muscles would have quivered and complained. They were stronger now and capable of long hours of vigil if need be, but a few minutes were all she had.

The solid wooden door cracked down the center with the first blow and was nearly split in two by the second. Whatever was on the other side was relentless, beating until the door finally caved into a mass of splinters. Portia stood at the ready, her Blessedwood ammunition laid out at her feet and the last scalpel shoved into her hair once more.

For a breathless moment, nothing happened. The pieces of the door lay where they fell, and the hallway beyond was so swathed in shadows that it seemed empty. Then, the low growling began again and the creature outside began to force its way through. The sturdy doorframe held fast at first, but soon it too bowed and broke, pulled

open into a gaping hole that tore large chunks of plaster free from the walls, showing the lathing beneath.

What shambled into the room was not what Portia expected. She had fought and slain demons of all kinds, but had never before seen a transformation like this.

"Nigel?"

The bulbous head swung toward the sound of her voice and four great eyes regarded her, each a different color: black, red, milky-white, and grey. The grey eye rolled in its socket, looking at her while the other three scanned the rest of the room. "Portia, sweet sister," it lisped through a lipless mouth of needle-like teeth. In that single gaze was all the cunning, malice, and avarice that had been in Nigel, multiplied a hundredfold.

Portia aimed as the massive, distended torso pushed through the broken doorway. She pulled the trigger. The bolt leapt forward and pierced the grey orb, spattering blackish blood across the slick and putrefied flesh. The thing that had been Nigel staggered back, keening, fumes billowing from the wound. It reached up with one hand full of multiple-jointed fingers and wrenched the stake free from the burnt and blistered flesh. It swung its head toward Portia and bellowed, spewing a rank vapor from its maw. The scars she had seen branded into Nigel's flesh were nearly invisible against the pale, puckered skin of his new body, but the tattoos stood out starkly. The glyphs seemed to undulate and shift as she stared, open-mouthed.

She fired again, aiming for the mouth, but the demon flung up a forearm, catching the bolt through the meat of the limb. The stake sizzled where it made contact, but the demon pulled it out and tossed at aside.

Two stakes gone, ten left of the dozen she usually packed. She would have to ration them carefully. She plugged one into the thing's left foot, and when it bent down to remove it, she sank another into its right shoulder. Ignoring the smoldering bolt lodged in its back, the demon advanced on her.

The bedroom door remained closed, and Portia wished Imogen would hurry up. A cartload of Blessedwood bolts might be enough to destroy the creature, but the eight she had left were not going to do much more than wound it. But she still had eight chances.

The fifth bolt was a shot to the groin that went wide, burying itself in the demon's thigh. It howled with displeasure and clawed at the deeply penetrated bolt. Portia loosed a sixth shot into its chest, aiming carefully to avoid the scars and tattoos. It plunged home with a spate of blood already beginning to form into purplish clots. The demon threw its head back and roared, sending a tremor through the room. Quickly, Portia dropped behind the chair and wrapped a bolt with some of the gauze. It took her three attempts to get a match to strike, but it finally flared and took flame in the wrapped cotton. She aimed for the body again, hoping to catch the clothing on fire. The bolt flew, the flames fanned into a fury by the passing air. It struck a glyph on the beast's stomach squarely and blew apart into slivers. Smoldering gauze and Blessedwood embers landed everywhere. She prepared another and aimed higher, hoping to strike the head. It flew true, eliciting another terrible and bone-rattling roar.

Portia surveyed the damage. Small fires began to catch

along one side of the room where the burning bits had landed on Nigel's books. The demon, for all its corporal wounds, kept advancing. It put its massive hands around the edge of the table and flipped it, sending Portia sliding to the floor in a jumble of stakes, books, and glass. She ducked beneath the wingback chair as it fell, shielding her body with it as the table came crashing down over her. She curled up around the crossbow and waited until the demon came looking for her. The table groaned as the creature lifted it, and Portia startled at the crack as it was thrown across the room, demolishing a curio cabinet and the potted palm in its path. The demon wrenched Portia's chair away. She fired, catching the thing under the chin with a bolt that left a ragged hole in its wake, destroying what had remained—despite the transformation—Nigel's incongruously patrician nose.

The demon arched back, both hands covering a face that gushed more fetid blood. But before Portia could re-load, something struck her hard in the chest. She recovered her breath and was aghast to see what was left of Nigel's shirt torn open and sprawling arms of flesh reaching for her. The greasy-fleshed writhing tentacles stretched out from two gill-like slits in the demon's sides. They struck out with amazing speed, landing blows and wrapping around her arms, wrists, hair, and finally her throat. She struggled to retrieve the scalpel, but her feeble cuts and shallow stabs did little to slacken the onslaught. The sticky mucous coating gave them a firm grip. Their touch burned bright and searing like the nectar of a sting-ing nettle.

One well-muscled appendage wrapped itself twice

around Portia's neck; the others held back her defense as the first began to squeeze. She gathered the light within her, and it began to glow through her skin. The echo began to sing and she along with it as the light grew brighter and brighter until it seemed Portia's flesh was that of a star, blindly and powerfully bright. The grasping appendages began to weaken and wither and finally to crack apart. She broke free of their suffocating embrace and staggered to her feet.

The demon had weakened considerably, but it was nowhere near defeated. It pushed itself to its knees, gatherings its strength as the tentacles still groped for her. The crossbow lay only a few yards from her, but she could not see either of her two remaining bolts. Her spent ammunition was somewhere in the flames across the room. Smoke thickened the air, and Portia grew light-headed.

"Nigel, what have you done?"

"No more shadows," he answered her. The words were garbled with blood and far too many teeth. "No more hiding. Only power. Only death. When I consume you, my last sacrifice, I will be complete."

"I won't let you."

"Then first I make my offspring on you, and after they are eaten, you will be next. You, I savor, my sweet, sweet sister. With your essence, I can wear the world around my neck like a jewel."

"No. By the blood and the soul of the Gyony, I will stand in your way."

"Gyony." He spat a curdled glob onto the floor. "Typical. Gyony will die first. All Gyony."

"No, we will not." Portia and the Nigel-demon turned

toward the voice with equal surprise. Imogen stood in the center of the room. Glyphs and sigils covered every inch of her naked skin, some drawn on in ink, others carved into her flesh and still dripping with fresh ruby blood. She shone with a celestial light and advanced on the demon, her red hair rippling behind her like a cloak.

She closed her eyes and the same kind of quiet ululation Nigel had made began in her throat. The glyphs on her flesh began to glow brighter, and the beat in Portia's breastbone quickened.

"Imogen, no!"

But her lover was beyond hearing. With arms outstretched, she opened her mouth to let the cries fly free. They filled the room and the demon that once was Nigel cowered a moment before diving into an attack. A sparkling field that surrounded Imogen rebuffed him.

"Dumah, thousand-eyed angel of death, you who command the silence and the stillness, you who hold the fiery rod of vindication, come unto me! Come with your legions of angels, come to punish this sinner!" Her body changed; her arms and legs grew longer, thicker, and her hair turned jet black. Great arcing wings, red as spilled blood, erupted from her back. In her hands, a flaming stave appeared. "I open my eyes onto you, Nigel Aldias, and to the demon souls in communion with you. I open my eyes and see your way into hell!" Imogen's voice was lost in the immortal thunder of the angel's. And as if a thousand radiant piercing eyes had indeed opened, the room filled with an unearthly light that made the hungry tongues of flame dull in comparison. Nigel screamed, straining his vocal cords to bursting.

Portia buried her face in the crook of her elbow, unable to look into the furious illumination. She could hear Imogen moving. The sound of her bare feet crunching through broken glass and splintered wood made Portia shudder. Chancing a glance upward, she saw Imogen, the stave afire in her hands, her eyes endless chasms of darkness.

I need to help her, Portia thought.

Help her, the echo reiterated.

Are we not one being now? One soul?

In reply, it whispered, *Are we not? I embraced you. But you have been afraid to lose yourself.*

I am.

Are you willing to let her die again? No one can save her this time.

What must I do?

Let me out of the confines you have created. Let me fill you and become you, for I already am you, Portia Gyony.

"I am Portia Gyony." She touched the center of her breastbone and dropped every magical defense she had been taught. The onrush of sensation brought her to her knees. The strength and the light that had surged through her when she called on it became the core of her being, indiscernible from her own memories, her own soul. And yet she remained herself, whole. "I am Portia Gyony," she repeated, and the world bent slightly around the edges.

She found that she could look directly upon Imogen without pain, without fear. Imogen, who was the vessel of Dumah, glanced in Portia's direction and nodded her head.

"Greetings, sister," she said, as if the light of death itself did not shine from her very eyes.

Portia inclined her head, giving deference to the rank she felt instinctively in the very marrow in her bones. Imogen turned back to her task and raised the great rod over her head. Nigel had collapsed to the burning floor, his broad shoulders hunched. He lashed out his clawed hands at Imogen, but his strength was fading. She drove the stave deep into his chest, shattering his breastbone and piercing his heart. Celestial fire burst from the wound and engulfed his body. Nigel howled and choked, his demonic body flailing in a desperate bid to survive.

Imogen stalwartly walked forward, her aura merging with the demon's. For a moment, there was nothing but a vast and brilliant corona. The ululation began again, this time higher pitched and faster, an urgent sound. But beneath it, Portia heard something else.

The faintest echo of her name. *Portia.*

She turned within herself for a moment, but the now-familiar presence was gone. No quasi-separate entity shared her body and soul. She felt whole, as if it had never been any other way. The voice whispered again, softly, *Portia.*

Within the sphere of light, a struggle and loud, keening wail were cut by the sharp intonations of that strange, lulling ululation.

Portia, help me.

She saw the shape of a human hand reaching toward her and she dove into the fray.

Inside that sphere, the world might as well never have existed. No room burned around them, no broken glass or splintered wood crunched underfoot. There was only light. And profound silence. It took Portia a moment to regain her senses.

Imogen lay at Portia's feet, naked and as still as the grave, and beside her was what remained of Nigel. His body was a broken shell, a twisted strip of flesh nearly devoid of bone and riddled with holes. The tattoos and scars were gone, leaving patches of skin that had the look of being scrubbed raw. His face was half gone, torn away by the force of a Blessedwood bolt. One eye was missing and the other stared blindly into nothing. His jaw, broken in several places, moved as if he were trying to speak.

Portia. The moan sounded ghastly now, grating and nauseating. *Portia, don't leave me.*

"There is no *you* any longer, Nigel. You gave it all away, and for what?"

He raised his ruined head, but the effort exhausted him and he collapsed. Portia glanced up into the face of the being that stood there. It was the face of death, of the abyss and the eternal silence of a sepulcher. She found that it did not chill her as she expected it might. Dumah stood a few feet away from her with the calm and impassive face of the dead.

"Take him," Portia said, nudging Nigel's broken body with the toe of her boot. "But this one is mine." She took Imogen in her arms and met Dumah's gaze, daring the angel to deny her. Dumah nodded and enveloped Nigel with blistered wings. The sphere of light vanished, leaving Portia's eyes dazzled.

It took only a moment for her to realize that the bright light was the hot flicker of fire. Flames completely enveloped the room. Portia stood in the center, dumbfounded as the conflagration raged around her and Imogen. She clutched her lover tightly to her. "It is going to be all right, I will get you out of here." But Imogen did not stir.

Heat forced Portia back several times before she reached the door. Behind her, the blaze consumed everything it touched. The notes and scrolls and books were nothing but smoldering embers. Portia slung her Gladstone satchel up over shoulder and decided to make a mad dash before the floor gave way beneath them.

Thick, black smoke choked the corridor, forcing Portia to crawl along the floorboards, dragging Imogen along with her. She made her slow, laborious way to the stairwell, where she could get to her feet once more and descend with Imogen toward the exit. Down, down she climbed, panting and bruised from her ordeal. Finally, she stumbled into the dormitory of the doomed children. The smoke still pervaded the air, but Portia felt they were out of immediate danger.

She settled Imogen against the wall and dug through her bag, finding the jar of smelling salts. Imogen was roused with a gasp and shudder. Her eyes were wild and unfocused for a long moment before she regained a sense of where she was.

"Portia," her voice was as dry as autumn leaves.

"I'm here, my love."

"Am I...? Am I *dead?*" She ran her hands over her bare flesh in awe. The glyphs and sigils were entirely gone.

Laughing, Portia told her, "No more or less than you were this morning."

"What's that smell?"

"We haven't much time."

"Is that smoke?"

"Well, yes. There was an accident with a couple of my crossbow bolts."

Imogen sat up and tilted her head. Her delicate nostrils flared and she listened. "There is no stopping the fire, is there?"

Portia shook her head. "I need your help to wake as many of the others as possible."

"Wake them?"

"If we are able. Either that, or we let them asphyxiate and die here."

Imogen shakily got to her feet. Portia slipped off her duster and helped Imogen into it. "Thank you," she murmured, drawing the cotton canvas around her and making her unsteady way to the first bed.

The electrical short Portia had begun in the specimen room had affected some of the machinery in this one. The smell of scorched wires was prevalent. Many of the children were already gone, drifted away into an endless sleep. Portia offered a prayer to Dumah to take their souls while she tended to the rest with smelling salts.

Imogen's beloved Molly and Sinclair slipped away gently into death as soon as they were removed from the strange machinery. Kendrick and Radinka came around, their deeply shadowed eyes squinted against the feeble light.

Imogen wrapped her arms around them, murmuring and humming, telling them to hurry and rouse the others. From high above, the floors collapsed in a splintering rumble. Portia was only halfway along the second aisle; only eight children stood on weak and wobbling legs. At least a dozen more still slept, and about twenty would never wake again.

"We have to get out, now." Portia began to round up the little ones.

Imogen wavered, swaying on her feet. "But the others...."

"Either we leave now with what children we have, or we lose them all and our lives as well."

"Give me just a moment longer." Imogen's tearful gaze paralyzed Portia. "Please, my love. *Please*. These are my sisters, my brothers."

"Go on, save who you can. You know the way out. I will take these little ones and head for the road." Portia reached her hand out for Imogen, who touched her fingers. They fell into each other's embrace. "I don't know if I can live through losing you again."

"Portia, you are the strong one, and you always have been. You are a Gyony to the bone: noble, fearless, beautiful."

"I'd hardly say that I was fearless." She laughed bitterly through her tears.

"Ah, but you'll agree to noble and beautiful. I love you, Portia." Imogen kissed her mouth hungrily. "I will be right behind you, I promise."

Portia gathered up the eight children, not one of whom appeared to be more than eight years old. But she knew better. Among them, she saw upward-tilting green eyes and silver hair.

The passage was agonizingly slow as the *Bene 'elim* children stumbled on atrophied legs. The large double doors that led from the main hall were painted shut, and Portia was forced to take them through the narrow passage that led to the chapel. She closed her ears to their cries of distress as they moved quickly down the marred center aisle and across the desecrated altar. She saw that her blood still saturated the top of it.

As she opened the door and began to usher her charges through it into the damp night, a gust of smoke and flying embers billowed into the chapel. The children shrieked and scrambled into the courtyard with Portia hard on their heels.

"Go toward the gates!"

Tumbling over one another and their own feet, the children obliged, running more or less for the arched gate. Portia stopped and turned, watching flames the size of great oaks lick through what remained of the roof. The ornate convent was already reduced to ruins. "*Imogen.*"

Behind her the children shivered and she turned away to tend to them. They stood in a cluster beneath the rusting arch, waiting. It would be a long walk down to the main road. She gave them a winning smile.

"Come on, my little ducks."

"Where are we going?" A steel-eyed boy with a lisp pulled at the hip of her pantalets. "Where's Imogen?"

"My name is Portia. I am Imogen's best friend and she bade me to keep care of you in her stead. We are going to a beautiful village not far from here called Penemue. It is where I grew up and where Imogen lived for many long and happy years."

They were only somewhat mollified, but followed anyway. Beyond the gate, the flagstone path ended abruptly in a patch of scrubby dirt. Lying there in the rocks and weeds was an apple, once a rich gold but now withered and rotten.

"Portia!" The voice was tremulous and thick with smoke, but she would have known it anywhere.

"Imogen? Imogen, we're here!" She ran back through the gate to find her beloved leading four children, all of them covered in ash and blood. The youngsters were so thrilled to see any of their fellows they did not seem to care to ask after the others. But the grieving would come soon enough. First, they would have a good meal and a hot bath in the safety of Penemue. She did not want to think of what waited for them there, whether Emile was safe and alive or if he had been dispatched by the treachery of the Aldias.

The children gathered where the flagstone path ended, looking anxiously down the hill to where the road, the buildings, and the flora all resumed. They fidgeted and whined.

Imogen limped toward them all, a broad smile on her sooty face. "I told you I'd be right behind you." She coughed and clutched her chest.

Portia slipped an arm around her, bearing her weight easily. "Are you hurt?"

"I didn't think so, but...I think something might be wrong."

"Wrong? How?"

"I am afraid...the spell...." Fear thrilled in her voice. She pointed to her bare chest streaked with ash and sweat.

"What do you m—?" The question died on Portia's lips. The flesh across Imogen's breastbone was unmarked.

"The magic is contained here." She nodded at the

burning convent and glanced uncertainly at the old gates. "I am not sure if I can leave."

Portia's mouth went dry. "No. Not after all of this. I *will not* lose you again."

"Portia, the choice is not yours."

She touched Imogen's chest, searching for the familiar *thrum* of the arcane symbol stamped onto her. She found it faint and faltering. "No, you are right. The choice is not mine. I can't make it for you." She stepped away, joining the waiting children beyond the threshold of the iron gates. She reached out her hand. "Come home, Imogen. We all need you."

Imogen stood with her bare toes just behind the line that divided what had once been their home, safe and hidden, from the wicked world that needed them to save it. And although she had faced down demons without so much as a flicker of an eyelash, she now stared terror-stricken at an empty swath of earth.

"I am afraid, Portia."

"Your body contained the Great Angel of Death tonight. You faced down Nigel and destroyed him. What else is there to be afraid of?"

"I don't want to die. *Again.* There is no necromancer to catch my soul and ensorcel it back into my body."

"You could stay here, I suppose."

"No." Imogen shook her head. "There is too much pain here. And my brothers and sisters will need me in the world beyond these walls."

"Then come." Portia plucked the silver Saint Christopher medallion from between her own breasts. She pressed it into Imogen's hand and closed her fingers over it. "May you not faint or fall on this day. I beseech you, Christopher, denied Saint, guide Imogen's steps, and allow her safe travel home again."

Imogen nodded and kissed Portia's hand, still clasped firmly over her own. "Take me home, my love." She closed her eyes and drew a deep breath. "Don't let go."

"Never," Portia whispered. "Never. I promise."

Imogen stepped across the barrier.

Acknowledgments

There are many people without whom this book would not have been possible. I would like to thank my husband, Matt, for being such a great partner in my life and in my writing. He is my meta-plot guru and helps me see the big picture like no one else can! I'd also like to mention my parents, my aunts, and my grandmother for fostering my creativity and letting me be the wild, eccentric child I was!

I never would have had the opportunity to play with this world had it not been for a party at Arisia with Michael and Nomi Burstein, Keith deCandido, and Jen Pelland. You guys are awesome, thanks for the support!

If I were to name everyone who helped me get to where I am right now, I'd need a whole other book, but someone I'd like to take a moment and express my eternal undying gratitude to is Jacqueline Carey. She is a great lady to whom I owe a great debt of gratitude. My only hope to repay it and do her proud is to be as successful as I can and bestow such time, energy, and kindness onto the up-and-coming authors that follow me.

And last but not least, the lion's share of all this goodwill and appreciation has to go to the Big Boss of Apex, Jason Sizemore. He's put a lot of faith in me and my writing, and more than just faith: he pays well, too! He has been the publisher every author dreams of having and I am grateful for this opportunity to be working with Apex every day. Thanks, Boss, I mean to do you proud, too!

Sara M. Harvey made her fiction debut in 2006 with the romantic urban fantasy *A Year and a Day*. In 2008, she turned her attention to horror with *The Convent of the Pure*, the first in a novella trilogy set in a steampunk universe.

Sara is also a costumer who works as an assistant costume designer and as an instructor in costume and fashion design. She has contributed to several costume history textbooks. She lives in Nashville, TN, with her husband and fellow author, Matt, and their dogs, Guinevere and Eowyn.

Visit Sara at her website: www.saramharvey.com.

As a longtime avid fan of the speculative fiction genre, **Melissa Gay** is at her most relentlessly perky when illustrating science fiction, fantasy, horror, or role-playing games. Her work has been featured on numerous covers and in the interiors of works in these and other genres, including scientific botanical illustration. Her passion is creating poetry in sweeping lines, bold shadows, and intriguing details. She looks to the works of illustrators, painters, and comic book artists such as Arthur Rackham, Alphonse Mucha, Don Maitz, Bernie Wrightson, and Bryan Hitch for inspiration and education. She will noodle with a finished painting until someone forcibly takes it away from her. ("I've just got to move this one line over five microns, then I'll put the brush down, really! Hey, gimme that back!") She received a B.A. in painting from the University of the South at Sewanee, Tennessee, and currently lives in Nashville with her husband and son.

Visit Melissa at her website: www.melissagay.com.

The Bram Stoker Award-nominated novella "Mama's Boy"
is the cornerstone of this 14-story collection from author,
Fran Friel, and Apex Publications. Packed with 280 pages
of demented, post-traumatic, brutally chilling horror,
these stories will linger. They will haunt. They will
accompany you into the night.

ISBN TB: 978-0981639086
ISBN HB: 978-0-9816390-7-9
www.apexbookcompany.com

unwelcome bodies

Separate your mind from your flesh and come in.
Welcome…

A collection of dark stories from one of the
leading female voices of SF, Jennifer Pelland.

LaVergne, TN USA
20 June 2010
186783LV00003B/40/P